SHOWDOWN

Ward Gale sprawled beside his dead horse and felt a desperate thirst. His shoulder bled where the bullet had seared the flesh. He raised his eyes and judged that the hot sun would not set for many hours. There was no hope in him, no fight left.

He had been ambushed and now the sniper was carefully biding his time. This was what he got for bucking powerful Matt Roberts—for pursuing Roberts over six thousand miles to avenge the cold-blooded murder of his brother. Suddenly, a twig snapped behind Ward. This was the showdown.

Todhunter Ballard was born in Cleveland, Ohio. He was graduated with a Bachelor's degree from Wilmington College in Ohio, having majored in mechanical engineering. His early years were spent working as an engineer before he began writing fiction for the magazine market. As W. T. Ballard he was one of the regular contributors to *Black Mask Magazine* along with Dashiell Hammett and Erle Stanley Gardner. Although Ballard published his first Western story in *Cowboy Stories* in 1936, the same year he married Phoebe Dwiggins, it wasn't until *Two-Edged Vengeance* (1951) that he produced his first Western novel. Ballard later claimed that Phoebe, following their marriage, had co-written most of his fiction with him, and perhaps this explains, in part, his memorable female characters. Ballard's Golden Age as a Western author came in the 1950s and extended to the early 1970s. *Incident at Sun Mountain* (1952), *West of Quarantine* (1953), and *High Iron* (1953) are among his finest early historical titles, published by Houghton Mifflin. After numerous traditional Westerns for various publishers, Ballard returned to the historical novel in *Gold in California!* (1965) which earned him a Golden Spur Award from the Western Writers of America. It is a story set during the Gold Rush era of the 'Forty-Niners. However, an even more panoramic view of that same era is to be found in Ballard's *magnum opus, The Californian* (1971), with its contrasts between the *Californios* and the emigrant gold-seekers, and the building of a freight line to compete with Wells Fargo. It was in his historical fiction that Ballard made full use of his background in engineering combined with exhaustive historical research. However, these novels are also character-driven, gripping a reader from first page to last with their inherent drama and the spirit of adventure so true of those times.

SHOWDOWN

Todhunter Ballard
&
James C. Lynch

GUNSMOKE

This hardback edition 2005
by BBC Audiobooks Ltd
by arrangement with
Golden West Literary Agency

ISBN 1 4056 8049 0

British Library Cataloguing in Publication Data available.

Printed and bound in Great Britain by
Antony Rowe Ltd., Chippenham, Wiltshire

1.

At sunset the ship had anchored in San Francisco Bay giving Captain Ward Gale his first look at that fabulous city, its shacks and its tents crawling up the steep hillsides above the water's edge. Here was the gateway to the gold fields of California. And this was the hour in which Gale had to decide how much longer he wanted to live.

Young and rangy, a man of strength and temper and big appetites and the will to control them, his natural bent was for the company of congenial men, but now he kept off to himself. Huddled in his greatcoat, he walked the boat's dark waist, pausing occasionally at the after break to look up at the ship's master pacing slowly back and forth and to remember his own lonely watches on other quarter decks. This was the first long voyage Gale had ever made as passenger.

As they had rounded up and dropped the hook, night had come and a thick, muzzling fog had closed in. The master, concerned and conscious of the Bay's dangers, cluttered as it was with abandoned shipping, had refused to land them until morning.

That was all right with Gale, but the rest of the passengers had come to dig gold. The impatience in them made hours out of minutes and kept them milling restlessly about the deck. And just when they had reconciled themselves to wait, a boatman had come out, offering them a chance to get ashore. Sitting straddle of the ship's rail, his left arm hooked through the bail of his guttering lantern, he stirred them up.

5

"Thirty-five dollars," he chanted. "Thirty-five dollars a man with what baggage he can lift. I can take two. Step up, gents. Plenty of rich claims right out of town, but you'll have to hurry. First ones ashore will get the best."

To the passengers, their eager minds inflamed by legends they themselves invented out of the meager details which had sent them west, the boatman's words held no absurdities. But some were already short of funds.

"Thirty-five dollars?" said a gaunt man. "That's a lot of money for a mile boat ride."

"Rich claims ain't going to last," the boatman said. "Men are pouring in. Tomorrow or the day after, those who come will have to pan and dig for it. Ground with gold lyin' in sight is gettin' scarce."

They hesitated, looking at one another. Then one pressed forward and the whole crowd moved. Gale was caught up by their urgency. Why not settle it tonight?

He drove his hard body carelessly through the crowd. They cursed him, but they got out of his way. He was too big for anyone to block and this sudden opportunity had robbed the group of any cohesion.

Gale shoved the last man aside and dropped a stack of coins into the boatman's greasy palm. "Here's a hundred," he said. "I'll go alone."

"Done." The boatman dropped quickly over the side.

Gale was after him, climbing the ladder downward toward the bogging skiff. A pistol slipped halfway from his coat pocket. He caught it, quickly, shoving it back. But the boatman had seen it and his dirty, stubbled face showed unease as Gale dropped into the bottom of the boat.

"Where's your baggage?" the boatman said, stalling. "You forgot it."

"Let's go," said Gale.

Above them the faces at the rail were envious and resentful and no one called goodbye. No friendships had been severed. Through the long voyage, Gale had kept his trouble to himself.

When the skiff pushed away from the ship, they were alone, walled in by the settling fog. Gale knew the sea too well to feel lost, but this could be serious. He sat facing the stern where the boatman stood erect and pushed his oars.

"You going to have trouble finding shore in this?"

"No," the boatman said. "Once you get San Francisco mud in your hair, you can smell it clean across the Bay. I foller my nose."

"So that's what it is," said Gale. "I thought it was gold I was smelling."

The boatman gave him an uneasy look. "You didn't swallow too much of my gab, did you, Red?"

"No," said Gale.

The man was still uneasy. "A good claim could be a mite farther out than I mentioned."

Gale smiled a little. "Stop worrying about the gun you saw. I'm not interested in gold."

"A man never knows," the boatman said. "To be honest, there ain't no gold right around San Francisco. In fact, since you ain't interested, I guess I can tell you it's a far piece out. And there ain't much layin' on top the ground, either. I didn't find any. You come here on business, did you?"

"Yes," said Gale. "Let's call it that."

"Must be important, the hurry you was in. You didn't quibble none on the price, either. Maybe I can help you."

"Maybe you can," said Gale. "Ever hear of a man named Roberts? Matt Roberts?"

"Captain Roberts? Sure. Everybody in California knows him. He a friend of yours?"

"I know him well. What happened to the ship he sailed? The Witch."

"He sold the cargo," said the man. "Then he sold the ship to Sam Brannan. Sam beached her. The Witch is a hotel now. Roberts is doing all right, too. He owns a big chunk of the country."

"So I've heard," murmured Gale. "Will I find him in San Francisco?"

The boatman shook his head. "Not tonight. His new river packet, the Cornucopia, is making her first run. Matt will be aboard. I saw him heading for the Embarcadero."

"An extra fifty," said Gale, quickly, "if you get me ashore before that packet leaves."

The boatman spat over the side. "Now that's my luck. She's left. I heard her whistle a spell back."

Gale swore under his breath. "Put me aboard her."

"Pretty risky in this fog."

"A hundred dollars risky?"

The boatman grinned, altering his course. "A hundred dollars easy. With this fog they won't be running fast. You must have important business with Roberts."

"I have," said Gale. "I'm going to kill him."

The boatman stopped rowing. "Kill Captain Roberts? Why Red, he's a big important man. They'll hang you for that."

"I suppose so," said Gale. "That's why I didn't bring any baggage."

2

The Cornucopia, newest and finest of the Roberts' San Joaquin river steamers, pushed swiftly through the fog toward Chipps Island and New York Slough, forty-five miles away. Gale saw her first. Her two high lights came out of the night with startling suddenness. He shouted his warning and the boatman turned, voicing his own fears:

"My God, she's coming fast!"

He dropped his oars and snatched up the lantern waving it frantically. "Hey!" he yelled. "Ahoy!"

Gale stood up. The packet's sharp, rising bow loomed incredibly over them, throwing a high, white wave right and left. It struck, cutting the skiff in two.

Gale, from his standing position, was hurled head first into the water. The weight of his greatcoat and the heft of the big pistols in his pockets dragged him deep. The cold water shocked the breath out of him.

Instinct made him fight up toward the surface and he came against the packet's bottom and was rolled over and over by the suction of the steamer's thirty-five-foot paddle wheels. He plunged down again until his head pounded with the beat of his own pulse, and he knew he had to have air or die.

The soaked heaviness of his coat hampered him and he tore desperately at the fastenings, ripping them free and fighting out of it. Thus lightened he shot to the surface, his head breaking through the crest of a heaving swell.

He gulped down air, tasting it, the salty fog flavor and the strong tang of vegetation dying along the tidal flats. Land tastes. Then he turned over, looking for help, for something to cling to.

The streamer seemed far away, her paddles slowing, their beat still audible and just now stopping.

"Wait!" he shouted. "Help!" The fog diffused the sounds he made, sending them back against his own ears.

Realizing he could not be heard, he started swimming with long, overhand strokes, seeing lanterns begin to wink on the steamer's engine deck, hearing the muffled, confused shouting of those aboard the boat.

The swim seemed endless; he had the illusion the steamer still moved or was poised to escape him. He redoubled his efforts. He had no fear of the water, but he had come too close to Matt Roberts to let him get away now.

Gale almost failed. As he came up to the stern and seized a trailing rope, signal bells jangled and the steamer started into motion, the wash forcing him back. The rope pulled taut. The small man holding it was jerked hard against the rail.

He let out a startled yell. The lantern in his other hand sailed out to hiss into the water beside Gale's head.

"Hang on!" Gale yelled. "Hang on!"

The rope slackened sickeningly, then tightened with a snap, almost loosening Gale's grip. Then the man on deck was shouting, "Help! Somebody lend me a hand."

Above the roiling sound of the gathering wake, Gale heard the pound of feet running on the deck. A harder strain came on the rope. They swung him in against the hull, lifting him from the water with unthinking suddenness. Just as his fingers broke loose from the slippery line hands reached down and grabbed his wrists. He was dragged aboard and held erect.

Gale pulled away from them and leaned back against the rail, drawing his breath in slow, even gasps, trying to quiet his pounding heart. News of the rescue spread and where a second before there had been only a handful of men, they now packed the deck, everyone closing in.

The small man who had held the rope tried to herd them back. "Let him alone," he begged. "Let him get his wind."

"You got the other one all right?" said Gale.

"Other one?" the small man said. "Was someone with you?"

"Sure there was," said Gale, and looked around vainly for an officer. "There were two of us. Let's get this packet stopped."

"You'll play hell doing that," the small man said. "They're out for a record run. The owner's aboard."

"They'll stop," said Gale, and pushed his way through the crowd to the nearest ladder. He swarmed up this to the pilot house, set cubelike on the texas between the tall, twin stacks.

There were two men at the big wheel. On the right hand side of the house a mate stood at the open window peering out into the fog. On the left the captain kept his lookout, his round head thrust aggressively forward.

"Ring her down," said Gale, sharply.

Long used to command, his tone made the mate reach instinctively for the signal cord. He caught himself in time and turned.

The captain swung around, lifting his black beard out of the upturned collar of his coat. His brown eyes, round as marbles and as hard, ranged over Gale in a long, all-including look.

"What's the matter with you?" he said.

"You ran down a skiff," Gale told him. "My boatman's not aboard. You going to leave the man out there?"

"What skiff?" the captain said. "And I don't like people running in here and telling me to ring my engines down. Get out of here."

"You going to stop?"

"No," the captain said. "We stopped long enough."

Gale hit him. The man smashed back against the bulkhead, then slipped limply to the floor. Gale dropped on him with his knees, laced his fingers in the man's hair and beard and beat his head against the deck.

Then he straightened quickly, ready for the mate. The mate stood motionless. The two helmsmen had not moved. The little man who had trailed that saving rope astern, stood wedged in the doorway of the pilot house holding back the crowd that had flowed up behind them. In his hand he held a pepperbox, a small but deadly gun.

"Take your time, Red," he said. "No one's going to interfere."

The mate looked at Gale. "It wouldn't do any good to turn back."

"Not now," said Gale. "I guess we'd never find him." He prodded the master with his foot. "But he could have stopped longer."

"He could have," said the mate. "He was running too fast in the first place. But we have the owner aboard and Captain Hames was hell bent for making a record. He's not going to like you when he wakes up."

"It doesn't matter to me," said Gale. "Where would I find the owner?"

"Don't try," said the mate. "You've had trouble enough for one night. I'll put you in a cabin and you can stay out of sight until we reach Antioch. Then you can go over the side and swim ashore."

"I didn't come this far to swim ashore at a place called Antioch," said Gale.

"I don't give a damn what you came for," the mate said. "I'll put you in a cabin. After that you can do as you please."

3

For a long time Gale stood motionless in the middle of the cabin. His energy was completely drained away and his bones ached from exhaustion. Even his desire to find Matt Roberts was momentarily gone.

After the cramped quarters of the sailing vessel this cabin was large and spacious and newly clean. A sperm oil lamp in a gimbaled frame spread its soft light over the glossy whiteness of the walls turning them to warm cream and making the gold leaf decorations glisten.

Against the far wall was a wide, double bunk. To the left a bolted down chest of drawers. To the right a small cabinet held a white bowl and its water pitcher. The floor was covered with soft carpeting and beside the door was a bench.

There was no knock. The cabin door opened and Gale spun around, lifting his hands, aggressively. It was the little man. He held a mug of coffee, smelling strongly of whisky, toward Gale.

Against Gale's sinewy bulk this man seemed frail. His features were regular and as delicate as a woman's, but without a woman's softness. His eyes were jet black, narrowed with the habit of mockery and his hair was dark and fine, growing down to a sharp widow's peak on his pale forehead. His mouth, mobile and red, showed quick humor and a fondness for cynicism, nicely balanced between laughter and cruelty.

"Drink this, Red," he said. "It will do you good."

Gale relaxed and took the cup. "Thanks. You've been a lot of help, tonight."

The little man cocked his head and smiled, shyly. "I always like to help an enemy of Matt Roberts."

Gale sipped a little coffee. "Who said I was an enemy of Matt Roberts'?"

"You."

"When?"

"Every time the mate mentioned Matt Roberts. But it's all right with me, Red. My name is Spencer Morehouse. I hate Roberts too."

"Why?"

"I don't know why. I just hate him."

Gale masked his face with the coffee cup. "You could be mistaken about me."

Morehouse laughed, silently. "Not me. I don't make mistakes. I'm a very observing man."

Gale finished the coffee and set the cup on the stand. The heat of the laced liquid ran down through his tired body, lifting and toning it back to normal reaction. His eyes ranged over Morehouse's well cut suit, his white linen and carefully polished boots.

"You going gold hunting in that outfit?"

"In my own way, Red. I never use a shovel or a pan." He came back to the former subject with a persistence Gale found irritating. "What's between you and Roberts?"

"Would that be any of your business?"

"I don't know why not," said Morehouse. "I saved your life. You wouldn't even be here if it weren't for me."

Gale raised his hand to acknowledge the debt and protest the reminder. Morehouse was suddenly four steps away, his pepperbox gleaming in his small hand. Slowly, a sheepish smile crept up into his dark eyes and he put the gun away.

"I beg your pardon," he said. "But when a man moves fast it startles me and you're pretty big." Slowly, he came back toward Gale.

Gale moved over and sat down on the bench, putting his elbows on his knees and letting his hands dangle. They were big knuckled, a little square and strong without being blunt. Sitting this way, he looked at Morehouse.

"I had a little dog like you, once. All nerves. You a gambler?"

"Me?" said Morehouse. "I never turned a card in my life. Why risk what you've got, to get something you might not get? Let's get back to Roberts, Red. Why do you hate him?"

Gale said, "Three years ago, in Boston, I borrowed money and built a ship and loaded her and sent her west. My brother sailed as master and my good friend, Matt Roberts, was her mate. One of the crew finally came back home. One night, standing in the dark, he'd seen Roberts smash my brother with a belaying pin and shove him over the rail. Roberts sold that ship and cargo as his own. That's how he got his start."

"I can believe it," said Morehouse. "That's Roberts. He's been stealing ever since, too. But if you've come for a settlement, Red, you'll play hell getting it. Roberts is too big and rich, now. He's entirely respectable. Besides this packet line, he owns the express run to the southern mines, and the stages. He owns a bank. All he has to do is lift his hand and he's got a hundred men to do his dirty work. You'll never get a dime out of Roberts."

"I don't want anything Roberts has," said Gale. "All I want to do is kill him."

"Kill him?" said Morehouse. "Why?"

Being essentially law abiding, Gale had to have an answer to that question to justify his position and his reason for taking this course. But he had never framed the reason into words. There were too many facets to it and he realized, for the first time, he had simply lumped them together into a thing called hate.

Had he been a devious man, Gale might have gone about this differently, but all of his twenty-seven years he had pointed himself directly at his goals. Now that the need for justice had come he saw no reason to change his ways.

So many people had been hurt by Roberts. Besides Gale's own deep, personal loss, there was the old lady he had boarded with. She had bought a share in the venture. Tim Sullivan, the inn keeper, had mortgaged his business to help lay the keel of the Witch. A hundred homes had felt the pinch of this loss. Peter Gale was dead and he had been too young to die.

He hardly realized he had been speaking aloud until the sound of his slow, solid words beat into his consciousness. ". . . so there's only one fit punishment for Roberts."

"Punishment, yes," said Morehouse. "But where's the punishment in death? You talk like a child, Ward. Who are you to say death hurts a man? You hit him with a bullet and, perhaps, he's better off than he is now. Who knows? Roberts hurt you and your friends. For that you want to hurt Roberts. But killing him isn't the answer."

Impatience boiled up in Gale. This decision to kill Roberts had been the last step of a mental process too intricately evolved to be turned aside by a stranger's platitudes.

"Words," he said. "Every time a man gets afraid of consequences, he falls back on words. I'm not afraid of the consequences of killing Matt Roberts."

Morehouse shook his head. "You keep missing the point. It's punishment you're working for. Now what will hurt Roberts most?"

"There's nothing a man wants to do more than live."

Morehouse flung his hands wide in disgust. "Where's your judgment? Roberts would risk his life for a thousand dollars. Life isn't what's dear to a man. It's what he owns that counts. A lot of men, who have lost everything, have killed themselves because of it. Use your head. Strip Roberts of everything he owns. Then if you're not satisfied, after punishing him, kill him. But that will only be doing him a favor."

Gale thought around in a circle and came back to the little man's logic. "That sounds nice, but Roberts is a rich and powerful man. All I have left is my hands."

"Hands," said Morehouse, holding up his own slim fingers. "Every one has hands. You use them to eat with and wash your face. It's your brains that count, Ward, and they have to be tougher than your fists. You don't have to be a big man to be tough in the head, either."

"Don't you have to be tough in the head to kill a man?"

"No. You just have to sell yourself a bill of goods. How easy was it to make up your mind?"

"Not too hard," said Gale. "A man hits you and you hit him back."

"In anger, yes. But anger cools off. You have to have a better reason after a long wait."

"I have. There's a hundred people who trusted me."

"Ah," said Morehouse. "That's not anger. You're building yourself up to be a martyr for their cause. You're willing to crowd back your ethics and all your training and pull a trigger. What's that get you? Any man can justify himself for one act. All you're doing is posing as an executioner. I know what I'd do if I were in your shoes. But then you probably haven't as much nerve as I have."

"No?" said Gale. "What would you do?"

"As long as I'm forgetting ethics, I'd forget them all. There isn't one thing I wouldn't stoop to do until I'd stripped Matt Roberts of everything he owns. In his case there isn't even any moral issue involved. He has no scruples. He killed your brother and robbed a hundred people to get his start."

Gale tried to fend him off. "What's your interest in this?"

"Beside hating Roberts, let's say I like you. Do you think you're the only man on earth who lives to see justice done?"

Gale shook his head. "There's nothing I can do but kill Roberts. To fight a man with money you have to have money. I haven't enough left to buy a meal."

A glow came into the little man's eyes. "Of course we need money. With money you can do anything. But don't worry about it, Ward. We'll take a quarter million apiece out of Carolina."

"Carolina?"

"It's a town," said Morehouse. "The richest square mile on earth." Excited, he took to pacing the cabin.

"Now get this picture. There are forty thousand men in Carolina, all of them digging gold. But it takes water to wash gold out of gravel. The boys at Carolina will pay anything for water. It's a dry camp. So we'll build them a water ditch. It can be done. The Stanislaus River is only five miles away."

"Forty thousand men," said Gale, "and no water to work with?"

"Oh, there's water," said Morehouse. "A man built a five mile ditch. But the richer the claims get, the more he charges for water. By the time the miners pay his water rates, he gets nearly all the gold that's mined."

"Who is he?" asked Gale.

"A man," said Morehouse, "by the name of Matt Roberts. I think you know him."

4

Gale had lived with his own solution to this problem too long to relinquish it easily. But this was a practical suggestion. He turned it slowly in his mind and unconsciously coupled it with his own desires.

"What would Roberts do if we built a competing ditch?"

"Turn the world upside down to stop me. Recruit a gang of toughs to fight us every inch of the way."

"And if the toughs couldn't stop us, would he come himself?"

"You're damned right he would. That ditch, without competition, is worth millions to him."

"Good," said Gale. "We'll build a water ditch."

"Now you're talking," said Morehouse. He crossed over and slapped Gale on the shoulder. "Together, we'll handle Roberts, all right. Now let's get some sleep. We'll talk about it in the morning." He shrugged out of his coat and hung it on a hook beside the dresser and then sat down to worry out of his tight boots.

"I didn't know I was butting in," Gale said. "When they showed me this cabin I thought it was vacant."

"Oh, you're not butting in," said Morehouse. "It's not my cabin, either. You think I'd pay Roberts for anything?"

Unembarrassed, he dropped his boots to the floor and rose to thumb his suspenders off his shoulders.

Gale had to laugh. "Incidentally, Spence, where will we be in the morning? Where are we heading?"

"That's a good question," said Morehouse. "This boat is going to Stockton. But the mate advised you to jump off at Antioch."

"We'll forget that," said Gale.

"Good," said Morehouse. He slipped off his pants and climbed into the bunk, bouncing on the mattress. "This is luxury. Roberts really put himself out when he built this one."

"It's fancy enough," agreed Gale. "What do they get for passage to Stockton?"

"Deck passage is eight dollars. I was going to sleep on deck and beat Roberts out of eight dollars. Now I'll sleep in here and beat him out of twenty-five. This bunk's wide enough for both of us." He moved over against the bulkhead and looked at Gale. "Come on and get in. Do your thinking with the light out."

Gale walked over and turned out the light. "See you later," he said, and left the cabin.

Outside, Gale stepped across the five-foot covered walkway and pushed against the rail. A steady rain was falling, washing the fog away. It seemed darker than ever, yet it was possible now to sense a restraining border against which this sluggish river flowed.

To Gale's right, water slopping from the churning paddle wheels made its constant cascading noise against the wooden wheel guards. The eccentric on the walking beam made its loblolly sound. The hiss of steam, the pressure hum of the boilers, the laboring suction of the pistons, all this blended with the drumming of the rain into a dull, annoying monotone.

It had been months since he had set foot on anything

except a wooden deck and all this was Roberts' fault. Thinking about it made Morehouse's words seem remote and Gale started moving, unconsciously, stumbling over sleeping men who mumbled their protests, being uncomfortable enough in the wet darkness.

When he came to the uncovered bow he paused and looked up at the pilot house. Roberts was not there and Gale moved on, swinging about the other side, and stepped into the garish saloon.

Here was light and gaiety and laughter; the smell of tobacco and whisky; the perfume of women who made these boat trips endlessly. The air was warm and pungent, the room crowded to overflowing, but there was no desire in him to share the gaiety. He was still looking for Roberts, and Roberts was not there.

Back in the outside darkness Gale paused to think, to wonder at a sudden feeling of relief. Was he almost afraid to meet Matt Roberts, afraid of what the meeting might lead to? It was hard to believe, since only three hours before he had paid one hundred dollars to travel one mile for no other purpose.

But in spite of himself he kept turning over Morehouse's words in his mind. There could be another way to punish Roberts, a way which would bring more unhappiness and pain than could a quick death. That was what Morehouse had intimated. Perhaps the small man was right.

Thinking about it deeply he turned down a passage between the cabins and walked through a path of light coming from an open cabin door, glancing in as he passed, what he saw not registering until he had progressed a half dozen steps.

Then he stopped, wheeled and went back to verify what he had seen.

He paused at the door, unobserved by the room's occupants. An old man lay stretched helplessly on the floor beside the cabin bunk. A woman bent over him, and for an instant, seeing only her back clothed in its green robe, Gale thought that she was one of the boat women, rolling a drunk.

Then he realized that she had her arms beneath the man's shoulders and was trying to lift him. Failing, she picked up the water pitcher from the stand and straightening, slowly poured the cold liquid down upon the man's face.

The water struck the bridge of the thin nose and coursed in rivulets down through the furrows of the cheeks to drip from the tufts of the thin white beard.

Gale laughed, and the laughter loosened some of the tightness which had bound him. It was, he thought, about the funniest thing he had seen in a long time.

His laughter turned the girl, and he had his first full look at her face. Her hair was nearly the color of his own, the eyes were green, the face clear cut, attractive.

The robe which she wore was only loosely belted at her waist, the collar's vee falling away to show a carefully molded neck, and the rising rounded swell of her breasts.

He caught his breath. He had never been unmindful of women, and this one would have attracted attention in any crowd. She stared at him now, caught motionless by the surprise of his presence, then quick anger came up to light sparks in her eyes and bring a full flush to her cheeks as she unconsciously drew the robe around her with a quick little gesture.

"Laugh, you fool. Have you never seen a man drunk before?"

Gale's laughter sank to a chuckle. "I've never seen one drowned by a water pitcher, and show no more response. I'm sorry, I didn't mean to intrude, but you'll have to admit that the way that water ran off his whiskers is amusing."

She glanced down at the man at her feet, lying quietly, his deep breathing unaltered, utterly unmindful of the bath which he had undergone.

"What am I going to do with him?" The appeal was not so much addressed to Gale but to herself. "I can't rouse him, and I can't seem to lift him. Usually he is partly able to help himself."

Gale smiled. "Let me." Without awaiting her permission he had stepped into the cabin, and bending, slipped his arm under the old man's shoulders.

Without conscious effort he lifted the light body to the berth, propping him in a half sitting position, holding him thus with one hand while he stripped the wet coat from the narrow shoulders. Next he removed the shirt, and then stretching the still sleeping man on the bunk he removed the boots and deftly covered him with a blanket.

He turned to find the girl watching him and smiled again. "Your father?"

She nodded.

"Don't worry about him," Gale told her. "Better men than he have lost their bouts with whisky. He'll be all right in the morning."

She studied him, still holding the robe tightly about her as if her small hands would offer some concealment. She noted that he was coatless, that his pants were wrinkled and not quite dry, that he was bare-headed and that his hair was tousled, and she guessed that he was a miner, heading back for the hills, his pockets empty after his San Francisco spree.

"Sleeping on a wet deck will not be pleasant," she said, "and I owe you something for your help. If you care to occupy the other bunk and keep an eye on father I'll be grateful. I'm in the next cabin."

Gale smiled, guessing at her mistake. "Your father will be all right, I think. I have my own cabin, although I thank you for the offer." He turned and would have passed her, had not she put out an involuntary hand to stop him.

"Wait, please, I'm sorry. I didn't mean to offend you. By your appearance I judged that you were down from the hills, broke perhaps and returning to the diggings. I thought you could use a little help in return for your kindness. Have you already made your strike?"

He was facing her, the faint smile still on his lips. "I'm not a miner, ma'am."

She stared at him. Most of her life had been spent among men, and she had thought that she understood them, but she found that she could not catalogue this big red-head. There was power in him, and an air of authority despite his makeshift dress.

"You . . . you're not in the army?"

He grinned suddenly. It had been on the tip of his tongue to tell her who he was, but he stopped. You did not tell a strange girl that you had come out to murder a man. You didn't tell her that if you ever expected to see her again, and suddenly Ward Gale knew that he wanted to see her again.

Maybe, he thought, it's merely the months that I've been at sea. Maybe it's the scanty clothes. It doesn't matter what it is or why I want her, but I do.

He did not think of it as love. He did not think of it as anything. He just knew that he wanted to put his hands on her shoulders, to pull her toward him, to feel the hotness of her mouth on his.

But he crowded down the thought, saying with forced lightness, "I'm not a soldier. I don't know what I am."

"But surely you know where you're going?"

He thought for a moment, and recalled what Morehouse had said. "Why yes, I know where I'm going. I'm going to a town called Carolina. I'm going there to build a water ditch."

She made no effort to hide surprise. "Carolina, why, I . . . but Carolina already has a water ditch."

His grin widened. He found for some reason which he could not quite explain even to himself that he was enjoying the conversation.

"So I understand," he said. "A water ditch, run by a thief."

The girl was staring at him, and he saw that there was a startled look in her eyes, that she suddenly seemed almost afraid. "Have you been talking to my father?"

It was his turn to be surprised and he glanced for an instant at the sleeping man on the bed. "Why no, I never saw your father before. I got my information from a man named Spencer Morehouse."

He was not prepared for her reaction for suddenly her green eyes changed, gaining an anger which was reflected in her voice. "So, you're tied in with that cheap little swindler. Get out of here."

Before Gale realized what she was about she had caught up the empty water pitcher and with none of the awkwardness that most women show in throwing things hurled it at his head.

Ward Gale had the reflexes of a trained fighter, and he ducked the water pitcher more by instinct than design. It struck the bulkhead behind him and shattered, spilling the slivers of white crockery across the floor.

Nor was she finished, for she caught up her father's cane and would have brained him had not he wrenched it out of her grasp, pulling her forward until he held her struggling in his arms.

"Behave."

The girl did not seem to hear. She battled fiercely, trying to break his hold. The tie belt around her waist worked loose and the robe slipped.

She stopped her battling and in that moment Ward Gale pulled her close to him. He had had no intention of kissing her when the struggle started. The thought had not even crossed his mind, but suddenly her upturned protesting face was only inches from his own, her lips were parted, and he brought his mouth down, full against hers. He felt her body stiffen in his grasp, felt her try to push him away, and then suddenly as if the strength had been drained out of them her arms were no longer pushing against him, and it seemed almost as if she were returning the kiss.

His arm slipped down, pulling her body against his. And suddenly they both realized that her robe was open. Embarrassment caught them both at the same instant and he stepped back as she pulled the robe quickly about her.

"Please," she said, "please," and her voice was no longer steady. "Please go."

Gale went blindly, fumbling his way through the door as if he could hardly see, and ran almost head-on into one of the boat women who had been standing in the passageway.

She stepped back, quickly, laughing at him. "What's the matter, Mister? Did she turn you down? Come on with me, I know how to show you some fun." She clutched his arm and turned toward the deck, but he shook free.

"Leave me alone."

She stared at him. "What's the matter, Mac? Too high-toned for us ordinary gals?"

He didn't answer. He turned and went quickly the other way, too shaken at the moment to think clearly, too shaken to think at all.

2.

LATER, STANDING AT THE RAIL, where none of the ships' lights could reach him, he thought slowly back over the events in the cabin. I'm crazy, he thought. I'm acting like a kid who has just found out what women are for. The girl down there is no different from any other. It's because I've been at sea too long. I've other things to worry about. I can't be worrying about a red-headed girl.

He turned, and saw a dark figure moving toward him along the deck. But the man did not come on. Instead he paused before the cabin where Morehouse slept and cautiously opened the door.

Gale watched, the short hairs at the back of his neck prickling a little. It could be Matt Roberts, hunting for him. But then the man spoke into the darkness and he realized his mistake. It was the mate.

"Gale. Gale."

Before Gale could answer across the intervening deck he heard Morehouse say, "Yes, what is it?"

"Antioch coming up in half an hour. Be ready to drop off the stern."

"Good," said Morehouse from the darkness. "How's Hames?"

"You damned near killed him." There was a lurking satisfaction in the mate's voice. "He had it coming, too, or I wouldn't be doing you this favor. Don't make a big splash when you go. If Hames thought he could get you, he'd run this bucket ashore, trying."

"I won't make a sound," said Morehouse.

"Good luck," said the mate, and walked toward the stern, away from Gale.

Gale let him go and continued to stand there waiting to see if Morehouse would come out to find him. When the little man did not appear, Gale let himself quietly into the cabin.

Crossing the floor, he felt the pockets of Morehouse's coat, searching for the small gun. It was not there.

Gale lit the lamp and moved over to the bunk. Morehouse's eyes were closed and his even breathing simulated sleep, but Gale was certain the small man was awake. Seizing his arm, he hauled Morehouse into a sitting position.

The little man squalled. "That's a hell of a way to wake a man. Where have you been? I've been looking all over for you."

"Have you?"

"Yes, the mate was here, wanting you to get off at Antioch. Now we've passed the damned place. You might as well come to bed."

"You're a liar," said Gale. "I was outside when the mate spoke to you. You didn't even make a try to find me and we haven't gotten to Antioch, yet."

Morehouse hunched his shoulders under the covers. "All right," he admitted, cheerfully. "I'm a liar. I don't want you to get off at Antioch. We got a water ditch to build."

"I'm beginning to wonder about that," said Gale. "I just met a friend of yours. A red-headed woman."

Caution came into Morehouse's black eyes. "A red-headed woman? Prudence Kellogg? How the devil did you meet her?"

"She was putting her father to bed."

"Oh," said Morehouse. "And she told you I got him drunk?"

Gale was evasive. "She said several things."

For the first time, since they had come together, Morehouse lost his glibness and seemed uncomfortable. "Don't believe anything she tells you. She's no friend of mine. But she is a friend of Matt Roberts." Worry came into his eyes. "You didn't mention the water ditch, did you?"

"What if I did?"

Morehouse grew more agitated. "Well, did you?"

"Yes."

"You fool! You fool! You fool!" Morehouse flung back the covers and jumped out of the bunk to pace back and forth, his thin legs showing white and spindly beneath the flapping tails of his shirt. He came to a stop in front of Gale, staring up at him.

"What are you trying to do? Warn Matt Roberts of our plans so he can have every bruiser in California waiting for us?"

"I didn't tell Matt Roberts anything," said Gale. "I haven't even seen him. What's the girl got to do with him?"

"Nothing," said Morehouse. "Nothing. She's only going to marry Roberts. Fools and idiots. I'm always blessed with fools and idiots and drunkards. I get the surest deal in the world. It's a natural. It can't fail. And what do I get for help? Fools and idiots and drunkards."

Gale gave a half step back. "What the hell is this all about?"

"Look," said Morehouse, drawing a deep, hard breath. "Just tell me exactly what happened."

Gale did. "And when I mentioned your name, she heaved a water pitcher right at my head. She nearly brained me."

Morehouse sat back down on the bunk and pulled the blankets around him. "Well, what are we getting excited about? Women always cause trouble. Prudence Kellogg has caused me plenty. Her father's a lawyer and an old fool. He likes to make speeches and the miners like to listen to him. He's probably the best loved citizen in Carolina town. But he can't let a bottle alone, once he gets started."

"So you helped get him started, tonight."

Morehouse chuckled. "It wasn't tonight. It was yesterday I started him. Once you get him going, he can't stop. I couldn't have him making a deal with those bankers."

"What bankers?"

Morehouse hitched himself into a more comfortable position. "Well, when I got the idea for a second water company, Kellogg was the logical man to put at its head. I talked to him and he agreed. But his daughter doesn't like me."

"Why not?"

Morehouse went right on. "So Kellogg broke with me and decided to promote a company himself. My idea had been to sell stock to the miners. But he came to San Francisco to raise money from the banks. I couldn't have that. If outside bankers came into Carolina, the miners would never invest in my company. I had to stop Kellogg. The easiest way was to start him drinking. No banker is going to loan money to a drunken man." He grinned at his own memory. "Now you see why the girl doesn't like me?"

"There are several things I don't see," said Gale. "First, why was the girl willing to have her father go ahead with a water company scheme but unwilling to have him associated with you?"

"I said she didn't like me."

"Also," said Gale, "she called you a swindler. You admitted, a moment ago, that you are a liar. Are you a swindler, too?"

"How do you mean?" said Morehouse, his eyes going a little blank.

"It's possible," said Gale, "to sell stock in a proposition without ever intending to go further. Was that your idea with the water company, Spence? Was that the reason she called you a swindler; the reason she refused to let her father tie up with you?"

Morehouse ran his right hand casually under the pillow and left it there. "Awhile ago, I asked you if you thought you were hard enough to put aside your ethics and hit Roberts with every possible method. You said you were. Have you changed your mind?"

"What's that got to do with this?" asked Gale.

"Everything," said Morehouse. "If you're hard enough, together, nothing can stop us."

"I'm hard enough."

The small man relaxed. "All right. I am a swindler. I never intended to build that water ditch. But I intended to sell a half million dollars worth of stock. It can't fail. Every miner in the country hates Roberts. They'll welcome a chance to strike at him. And, also, lower their water rates. Are you with me?"

"That's no deal," said Gale. "Where does it hurt Roberts?

All you have is a cheap, crooked scheme to hurt forty thousand miners."

"Now wait a minute," said Morehouse. "If you're going to break Roberts, you're going to have to look a long way ahead. A while ago you said it would take money to break him. I'm offering you a chance to make that money. What do you care where it comes from?"

Gale moved away and sat down on the bench. He was certain now that Morehouse was not the least bit concerned about any revenge on Matt Roberts. The little man was only interested in easily made money and he would use anyone he could to further his own ambitions. At the moment, Gale's hatred of Roberts was made to order for his scheme.

Debating, Gale wondered if, by some chance, he could use the little man's conniving to break Roberts. Up until now he had been driven by an obsession to kill and get it over with. But if he were going to take this other way, he would be a fool not to use the weapons at hand. Yet he could not decide. He had not made up his mind quickly in the first place and this new decision could wait until he knew more about Morehouse and his methods.

He looked at Morehouse and said, "Maybe I don't care. We'll talk about it in the morning." He got up and crossed the cabin and turned out the lamp.

While he undressed in the dark he heard Morehouse twisting and turning and knew the little man had been made nervous by his apparent lack of decision. Gale made a note of that and smiled a little to himself.

2

Daylight, chill and dull and grey filtered through the cabin windows when Gale came awake. Wind gusts rattled the door and occasional squalls of rain beat in against the sash.

Gale stretched and rose. His clothes were dry, but stiff and wrinkled. He moved to the stand and washed with a morning vigor Morehouse found distasteful. Spencer lay there, wide awake and alert, the blankets pulled up under his chin, watching.

"You're a healthy animal," he grumbled. "Come on back to bed and keep warm. We won't be in Stockton for three hours."

"That's too long to wait for breakfast," said Gale, ruffling his red hair, before the mirror. "Get up. I'm hungry."

"Breakfast!" Morehouse sat up. "Are you crazy? You're supposed to have dropped over the rail at Antioch. You better pray that no one finds out you're still aboard."

Gale turned and looked at him. "You don't think I'm going to hide here, do you?"

"You will unless you're altogether a fool. Not only Hames would like to lay hands on you, how about Roberts? You came out here to kill him. He's already killed your brother. Do you think he'll just stand there with his hands in his pockets when he sees you? You haven't even got a gun."

"You have, Spencer. What would happen to your water ditch if Roberts killed me?"

Morehouse jumped out of the bunk. "You mean you're going into it?"

"I'm still thinking about it," said Gale. "But you better not take any chances. Come to breakfast with me. If Roberts sees me, and pulls a gun, shoot him. That will be all right with me."

Quick anger darkened Spencer's black eyes. He was being used and he knew it and he did not like the idea. "Maybe I ought to let Roberts kill you," he said. "Maybe I ought to kill you myself. That would make Roberts a friend of mine."

"You won't," said Gale.

Muttering to himself, Morehouse took his time to dress, straightening his coat with meticulous care. When he retrieved his small gun from beneath the pillow, he examined it carefully before dropping it into his coat pocket. Then, with an air of resignation, he followed Gale onto the walkway.

The boat ran now on the crest of a yellow flood that curved and twisted through a soaked land. There were no true river banks. Water spread out across the willow-lined shore, making small, muddy islands, mere humps rising out of the eddying currents and shallow swamps.

At the moment the rain had let up, but the sky remained a leaden arch, solid and threatening, turning everything below it drab and glossless and uninteresting. Sleepers still huddled on the wet boards of the deck, moaning profane protests at the rawness of the day.

Gale felt sorry for them, but Morehouse paid no attention. Stepping almost daintily around the mounds of baggage, he picked a path to the dining saloon.

The big room was furnished in the latest fashion, the windows curtained richly with red plush caught stiffly back with gold, rope ties, tasseled and ornate. The settees along the wall, in matching plush, were bolted in position, as were the white covered tables.

All this made no impression on Gale. He saw Roberts, instantly, and went cold, wrestling with the urges that had built up in him all these long months. Big and bulky and handsome, the man sat at the head of the captain's table. Gale knew a momentary satisfaction that the captain was not there, then all of his bitter interest came back to Roberts.

Here was a man who had been his friend, a man his judgment had forced upon his brother. Gale looked for some change in the full, florid face. Surely a man who had turned his back this far on what he had once been, would have changed. But there was no outward sign of it.

Roberts was smiling, animated. Prudence Kellogg sat at his right and Gale had the impression that her face, in repose, was even more beautiful than he had imagined. Across from her, her father sat silent and listless, a little sunken. His hands shook as he raised his coffee cup.

Gale brushed down Morehouse's restraining arm and walked directly over to pause behind the vacant chair at the girl's side. "Good morning," he said.

Prudence Kellogg looked around, startled. Seeing him, color came rushing up into her cheeks. Roberts looked up, his full lips still formed in their smile, but the humor shocked out of him. His face grew stiff and ugly, and white lines ran down from the corners of his nostrils. Then, with a studied casualness that must have cost him heavily, he looked back at the girl.

"You were saying, Prudence. . . . ?"

Morehouse, alert, had taken his position at the lower end of the table, facing Roberts. He stood motionless, waiting for the play.

Gale said, "Good morning, Miss Kellogg," and sat down.

Across the table, Wilson Kellogg, puzzled, put down his coffee cup. The girl's color heightened. Seeing this, Roberts showed his first trace of real annoyance and this pulled his attention back to Gale.

Gale's smile was meaningless. "How are you, Matt?"

"I'm sorry," said Roberts, measuring him. "I don't believe I know you." He looked back at the girl, as if he groped for his position. "Do you know him, Prudence?"

"We're old friends," said Gale.

Prudence stiffened and turned to Roberts. "I know nothing about him except that he is on his way to Carolina to build a water ditch. He said he was a friend of yours."

"He lies," said Roberts, flatly. With that he raised his bold grey eyes, putting the next move up to Gale.

"All right," said Gale. "Let it go."

Spencer Morehouse moved down the other side of the table to pause beside Kellogg. "Good morning, Wilson. I don't think you've met Ward Gale. He's my engineer. He's well acquainted with conditions in Carolina and has agreed to do something about them."

Interest flickered up in Kellogg's tired eyes. Sober, his legal mind was one of the shrewdest in the state and he had missed the byplay between Roberts and this stranger. There were things beneath the surface here that had not yet come up.

Essentially an honest man, Kellogg disliked Roberts and his ruthless methods. As a father he feared this same ruthlessness in relation to his daughter and it tormented him to know that all he had to do to make things easy for himself was to compromise his principles. He dreamed constantly of a career in politics. With Roberts' backing, this could be easily accomplished. It was to Kellogg's credit that he would grasp at straws rather than take this smoother, surer way. Gale liked him, instantly.

Kellogg rose and reached his hand across the table. "This, sir," he said, "is indeed a pleasure." He was incapable of speaking without an orator's pompousness. "Indeed a pleasure, sir. If you are aware of the situation in Carolina, you are aware of one of the greatest injustices of . . . ."

"Father!"

Kellogg let his words trail off, completely dominated by his daughter. He lapsed into embarrassed silence and sat down. Morehouse took the chair beside him.

For Roberts' sake, Gale enjoyed the consternation his presence caused. Roberts having put the next move up to him, it pleased him not to make it. This way was better. He wondered what Roberts would have done had not the girl been there. Roberts had held his control well enough, but he was obviously disturbed and uncertain in the face of Gale's apparent acquaintanceship with the girl. That was something to remember.

Morehouse said, "Now that you have failed to interest the bankers, Wilson, wouldn't it be wise if you joined forces with Mr. Gale and myself?"

Prudence Kellogg pushed back her chair, rising, her voice icy. "I've told you before, Mr. Morehouse, that my family wants nothing to do with you. Come, father."

Wilson Kellogg mumbled something into his napkin and rose. Roberts followed him and put a possessive hand on the girl's arm. But before he moved away, he said across his shoulder, "You may find it hard to get to Carolina, gentlemen. Stockton's full of miners waiting for the road to dry. I don't believe you'll find seats on any stage."

3

Returned to the cabin, Morehouse dropped onto the berth and nursed his displeasure.

"You and your damned appetite. You couldn't wait until Stockton. Oh, no. You had to go down there and make a fool of yourself. What did you accomplish?"

"Enough," said Gale. "Roberts is worried. Worry doesn't do a man any good."

"Matt, worried?" said Morehouse, scoffing. "He even denied knowing you and he almost convinced me. Do you think other people will believe your story?"

"I don't care what other people believe. Matt's a good

actor. But underneath, he's worried. He doesn't know how much I've told the girl. That will worry him. I didn't mention my brother, the Witch or anything. He isn't even certain how much I know. That will worry him. You were right, Spence. This is better than killing him."

"Sure," said Morehouse. "All you have to worry about is him killing you, now. He's warned. The girl brought up the water ditch. I had to talk about it, then. It's better to talk about something than to try and hide it, once it's out in the open. You better decide to go ahead with me, Ward. In this country, a man is on one side of the fence or the other. You're going to need all the help you can get."

"We'll see," said Gale. "I haven't made up my mind, yet."

"Then I'm done with you," said Morehouse, rising. "I'm not going to hurt my chances by getting involved in your fight with Roberts."

He reached for the door and it opened in his face. The mate stepped in, backed by two deckhands armed with rifles.

"Well, Mister," the mate said, looking at Gale, "you can't take advice very well, can you?"

Gale said nothing. Morehouse was poised, rigid, waiting his chance. It never came. The rifles were unwavering, deadly. The mate said, "My orders are to search you both."

He moved behind Gale and ran his hands over him. "All right," he said and moved on to Morehouse, making his search as thorough. But he failed to find the pepperbox and Gale was surprised.

"All right," the mate said, again.

Morehouse's eyes were muddy and unreadable. "What happens now?"

"I don't know," the mate said. "My orders are to lock you in this cabin. Don't try anything. These men will be outside."

He left. The key clicked definitely in the lock and Gale waited for the little man's outburst.

Morehouse sat down. "It looks like," he said, thoughtfully, "both of us have been arguing needlessly. We'll never get to Carolina, now. You and your damned appetite. Fools, idiots and drunkards weren't enough. Now I can add pigs."

"You can add that big mouth of yours," said Gale. "If I

hadn't listened to you, last night, I'd have killed Roberts."

Morehouse reached down inside his belt. He found a string and, pulling on it, lifted the pepperbox out of his pant leg.

"I," he said, flatly, "may have to kill somebody, myself, to get out of this jam. And I'm not going to be particular about who it is."

3.

THE PORT OF STOCKTON was built on a swamp, its embarcadero reclaimed from green tule bogs. Every sort of stuff had been used for fill, drift logs, abandoned freight, all the debris of the wild migration. It sprawled, rank and foul, a muddy monument to man's everlasting stubbornness.

Not even Captain Weber had anticipated the mushroom growth of his town. But it was in a natural geographical position on the low river bank where the through travel route left the stream and cut southward toward the southern mines and the settlements beyond.

Unlovely in the best of times, it was a madhouse now, filled to the bursting point with impatient men. Its shed-like warehouses were crammed, its docks were loaded and piles of uncovered goods sank rotting in the wet.

The upper town was in no better shape. The raw plank and canvas buildings along the rutted mire of Center Street were not sufficient to house the stranded travelers held in this hilly hole by the unprecedented rains and the bottomless mud of the curving road to the south.

Men slept on floors, on cots and in the filth of alley mouths. By day they surged restlessly from one dive to another, from one plank bar to the next. Food was short, but the supply of whisky was inexhaustible. Men brawled and drank and fought and stared in sullen boredom at the leaden sky, waiting for the sun.

The arrival of each fresh steamer made the only break in their monotony and the Cornucopia's plume of smoke, rising over the swamps, emptied the bars, silenced the tinny pianos and stilled the shrill cries of the girls.

Like rats coaxed from their holes, the population poured into the street. Men slouched toward the water front in phalanx which jammed the thoroughfare from building line to building line, until the embarcadero was filled with a solid crowd turning their bearded faces upward toward the steamer's decks, their hoarse voices shouting greetings and obscene advice.

From inside their cabin, Gale and Morehouse heard the swell of sound and moved to the windows to have their glimpse of the sorry town and the crowd below. Gale noted everything, seeing all this for the first time, but it was old to Morehouse and he was only interested in a few details.

"There's Ben Derksen," he said. "The fat fellow standing by himself. Over there against the mud wall."

"Who's he?" said Gale, with little interest.

"My driver," said Morehouse. "I left him with the wagon and team. You've got to guard horses in Stockton. They'll steal them right out from under you. If we could attract Ben's attention. . . ."

Gale saw a huge, round man planted against a crumbling, mud wall, a human barrel of a man who seemed to put a strain on anything he leaned against.

"What would move him?" said Gale.

"Don't let him fool you," Morehouse said. "When he wants to, Ben can move. He was with Taylor in Mexico. I've seen him lift a barrel of beer over his head and toss it thirty feet."

But Derksen was too far away and Gale's interest shifted from him. Outside, the two guards were jostled as men streamed past, eager to get ashore. They flowed down the gangplank in a surging, bundle-laden stream. Gale had an impulse to smash the glass and call out to them, but remembering the men he had left behind him, in San Francisco Bay, he knew these gold seekers were too intent on landing to pay any attention to another man's troubles. He turned, finally, and sat down on the bench, not one to waste his energies on futilities.

It was almost an hour before a key rattled in the lock and the door opened. The mate said, "All right. You can go ashore now."

"Just like that?" said Gale.

"Just like that," the mate said.

Morehouse stepped ahead of Gale and moved onto the deck, reaching the rail and looking down. "Oh," he said. "So that's it."

Gale moved to his side. A huge man stood at the foot of the gangplank, blocking it, staring up at them, his broken teeth showing as he smiled through a stubble of black beard.

In spite of the cold drizzle, his shirt was open almost to his belt, showing the thick mat of his chest hair. His left ear was puffed and wrinkled, standing out thickly through his unkempt hair. Behind him, a half dozen men made a semi-circle, obviously for his support. The dregs of the crowd idled beyond, watching, waiting hopefully, as if guessing what would happen.

"Who's the ox?" asked Gale.

"It's Peter Chauncey Burns," said Morehouse. "A professional bruiser. He works for Roberts."

"Good?" asked Gale.

"He's licked Yankee Sullivan, twice. Once in the ring and once out of it."

Behind them the mate said, "Still going ashore, Mr. Gale?"

Gale turned to grin. From the corner of his eye he saw Spencer's small hand move out of sight into his coat pocket.

"Not that," said Gale, quickly. "Come on."

Lightly, he dropped down the ladder to the engine deck and moved along it to the sloping, cleated plank. Morehouse muttered at his shoulder.

"I can hit his belt buckle or his left eye from here. Once we make it to my team, they'll never catch us."

"No," said Gale. "Save that gun for Roberts."

Gale paused then, looking behind him and upward. Two coated figures stood at the edge of the texas. One of them was Roberts, the other Captain Hames, his bare head showing a circle of white bandage. Though Gale looked at them, both men pretended not to notice him. He knew, then, this was no accident, and started down the plank.

"All right, Burns," he said. "All right."

Gale had not led a sheltered life and he recognized the signs when Burns spat and grinned and settled himself. He had no real fear of the man alone. His early years at sea had conditioned him and brought him into close bodily contact with other men like Burns. What he did fear were Burns' confederates against his back; there were too many of them for Morehouse, even with his gun.

But he knew how these things went. If he could catch the interest of the lingering crowd, if he could turn the fight into a sporting event, then the spectators would assure him fair play.

"You think you can keep me from landing, eh Burns?"

"I'll run you back on board with your tail between your legs."

"A hundred says you can't."

Greed lighted Burns' eyes, and cruel eagerness. "Let's see your money, sport."

"Morehouse has mine. Give him yours to hold."

Burns hesitated and Gale mocked him. "What's the matter? A hundred too much for you to lose?"

The big man licked his coarse lips, pulled a small pouch from his pocket and tossed it to Morehouse. "Watch the little feller, boys. I'll collect from him when I kill this redhead."

The crowd closed in now and Gale did not wait. He took the last two steps on the run and whipped his left fist into Burns' face. The big man sat down in the mud.

His friends tried to rush in, but they were caught by neutral spectators and hauled back. Men quickly formed a rough ring, shouting, "Fair fight! Fair fight!"

Burns struggled to his feet, shaking his head, and fell into a prize ring stance, his left arm extended, right arm bent up at the elbow, his chin held back.

Gale had no intention of fighting Burns' own way. He danced in, his fists held close, his shoulders hunched to protect his chin. He flicked a sharp, jolting punch into Burns' mouth, moving sideways and away as the blow landed.

Burns missed a savage swing and pivoted heavily to meet this strange attack. Angered like a tormented bull, he roared and lashed out again. His knuckles ripped Gale's shoulder flesh.

Gale's return smashed wickedly on that bent ear, jarring the heavy skull. It stopped Burns, but pain laced up Gale's arm as his knuckles split, turning his stomach sick and his knees weak. He was saved, for the moment, only by the fact that Burns was staggered. Then Burns came in again, his long arms sweeping like scythes. He landed twice before Gale could tie him up, the rock-like fists jolting with cutting force.

Using his crippled left arm as a hook, Gale partly smothered the next attack. The shouts of the crowd made a dull roar. Heavy whiskers scratched his face. Burns' breath was rank with whisky and tobacco. It belched out each time Gale's left fist hammered into the man's short ribs.

Burns wrenched to free himself and failed. Lowering his head, suddenly, he used it as a ram to butt Gale in the mouth.

Gale exploded. The pain of his smashed lips drove out reason and restraint. He beat and pounded Chauncey Burns and never knew the return punishment he took nor felt the pain of his ruined hand. His shirt was torn away, his body lacerated.

In the end it was condition that won. Gale was younger. Burns went to his knees from exhaustion, burying his face between Gale's legs. Even in this position, Burns tried to upset his red-headed tormenter. Gale stepped back and brought up a knee and Burns slid forward into the mud.

For a moment Gale stood over him. Then, turning, he glanced up to where Roberts stood. That done, not caring, he walked numbly through the parted crowd and reached the foot of Center Street.

Here Ben Derksen moved away from the wall of Pont's Saloon and took his arm as Morehouse came up.

"Why that was a fight," the fat man said, and smacked his spongy lips. "I guess I never saw a fight like that before. Who is he, Spence?"

Morehouse was shaken. Looking at Gale's battered face,

he said, "What was the idea, Ward, of making me hold the bet? How did you know I could pay if you lost?"

"If I had lost," said Gale, "that wouldn't have made any difference. We'd have both been back on that boat and lucky if we ever saw San Francisco. Which reminds me. Where's that hundred I won?"

Morehouse held back. "We're partners, aren't we?"

"Not yet," said Gale.

"All right," said Morehouse. "How you going to get to Carolina? You think Roberts will let you ride one of his stages? No. And you can't ride to Carolina in my wagon unless we're partners."

Gale managed a grin. "I tell you what." His voice was stronger now, his breathing less labored. "You keep the money and give me a ride to Carolina."

Morehouse nodded quickly. "That's a deal. And·we'll start right now before Roberts thinks up something else to do. Get the team, Ben."

"Well, I'll tell you," said Ben Derksen, shifting his big weight from one foot to the other. He removed his broken hat and pointed to a huge knot on the side of his round head. "See that? I went to sleep in the wagon, the other night. When I waked up, the wagon was gone." He hitched his gun belt with a certain dignity and sent tobacco juice out in a brown jet to splash against the mud.

Morehouse looked so dumbfounded, Gale burst out laughing. He said, "I can't ride in your wagon if you haven't one, Spence. Give me my money. At least I can get some clothes."

Morehouse, paying no attention, danced in front of Derksen. "You dumb ox! What's the matter with you, anyway? Now we're stuck. We'll never get out of Stockton and it's all your fault."

Derksen gave his belt another hitch. "Why, if you don't like it, Mr. Morehouse," he said, "the next time you go to San Francisco, you can stay in Stockton and watch your own team."

"No use getting sore," said Gale. "Give me that money."

Reluctantly, the small man slid the gold into Gale's hand. "What about our water deal?"

"I haven't made up my mind, yet," said Gale. "Find me a way to get to Carolina and I'll talk to you." He turned, without another word, and plodded up the center of the muddy street.

2

Gale came out of Leobetter's store, carrying a bulky package, and angled across toward Henn's Shaving Parlor. Men had already drifted back from the landing, filling the board walks in little groups or wading aimlessly through the muck. They paused as he passed, watching him with silent awe.

Behind the barbershop was a homemade shower, a bucket hung between two uprights, from a cross bar. Below it was a grating made from slippery slats, covering a tub of water.

The water was not entirely clean. You filled the bucket from the tub. You stood on the slats, shivering and naked, and let the water, running out of the perforated bucket, course down your back. A piece of tattered canvas offered a certain privacy, but it was too badly torn to make much protection.

Gale paid his dollar and received a chunk of yellow soap. He stepped into the yard and stripped. Then, filling the bucket, he stood under the trickling stream and soaped himself thoroughly.

His hand was puffed and throbbing and the lye soap ate at his cuts and bruises, making them sting. But the cold water brought life to his aching legs. It took three full buckets to rinse his body, then he dressed.

The town had offered little in the way of finery. A miner's red shirt was the best he found and a pair of butternut pants, at least clean. His boots he kept, but he added a belt and a single pistol to his outfit.

Thus dressed, he stepped back into the shop and let the barber's scissors shorten his hair and the razor scrape his battered chin.

Returning to the street, he sought the nearest bar. The whisky found the cuts inside his mouth, searing them with its sharp, antiseptic touch. Several of the drinkers spoke to him. He nodded, vaguely, wondering how they knew his name and not much caring. He was hungry as it neared noon and he found a place to eat, dining on venison, flat, soggy biscuits and a helping of beans.

With a cigar between his teeth he left the restaurant and leaned against the plank wall, outside, considering and trying to reach a decision. He felt pulled this way and that. Ever since the Cornucopia had struck the skiff, in San Francisco Bay, he had gone off on tangents rather than press closer to the hub of his first plan. Now, viewing the crowded street, the men hurrying nowhere and the endless mud, he felt helpless. He wondered where Roberts might stay in a place like this. He wondered what had become of the girl. Morehouse might know. It irked Gale to feel so dependent, but he pushed this down, starting along the street.

As he did so, four men fell in behind him, making no pretense to hide the fact. Across the street, a half dozen more kept steady pace, looking over at him. Gale stopped and turned quickly and walked back against the four on his side. He said, "Hello, boys."

They grinned and one said, "Howdy, Red. That sure was a trimming you gave Burns. The boys at Moke Hill or Hangtown would have paid good to see that one."

"An idea," said Gale. "But I thought that because I'd licked Burns, somebody might be following me to get even."

"Don't worry about that, Red. That's what we're here for."

Startled, Gale looked at each one. Then he smiled, not quite understanding. "All right," he said, and went on, the four keeping step behind him.

Moving this way up the street, his following increased until he reached the hotel. He paused, again, looking inside.

Here were none of the comforts of the river steamer. The place was sparsely furnished with makeshift things, temporary and spartan in their plainness. A high desk backed up against the stairs. Behind it, a square keyboard held twenty hooks. Beyond that, through an arch, he had a glimpse of the dining room, long and narrow, almost filled with a center table, this table bare except for a double row of tin plates faced down against the flies.

Gale had a momentary view the full length of the two rooms. At the far end of the dining table, Spencer Morehouse sat with a book spread open before him and there were piles of gold at his right elbow. Wondering what game the little swindler played, Gale moved in through the crowd.

Morehouse was saying, "Any more? This chance won't come again. Stock is half value, now. Once we reach Carolina, the shares will be a hundred dollars each."

Apparently the crowd was already milked. No one else approached the table. Instead, the men in the room turned their elation on Gale. Several of them pressed forward to slap his shoulder. One, made lean looking by an enormous beard, said, "Our money's on you, Red. You'll lick Roberts the same way you took Burns."

"What's this all about?" asked Gale.

Morehouse spoke sharply. "That's all, boys. Ben, clear the room. We'll have a business conference."

Gale had not seen Derksen standing to the right of the entrance. The fat man moved out now and breasted the crowd, expertly forcing them toward the lobby. When the last man was gone, he closed the doors and put his back against them.

"All right, Ward," said Morehouse, then. "Come on and pitch in." He waved a hand almost disdainfully at the gold. "It's half yours."

Gale walked over and stared down at the small fortune. "How did we get it?"

"We got it by selling stock in our water company. The Miner's Mutual Water Company of Carolina."

"Not we," said Gale. "I haven't agreed yet. I haven't made up my mind."

"I couldn't wait for you to make up your mind," said Morehouse, smiling. "I made it up for you. You might as well take your cut. You're running half the risks."

"No," said Gale, roughly. "I make up my own mind. When I do I'll let you know."

"You're my engineer, Red, whether you make up your mind or not. Ben's been spreading the word all over town. The boys are snapping at the bait. They like the way you handled Burns."

"Spence," said Gale, "you're not even smart. What makes you think I'll stand for a deal like this? I'm going out on the street, right now, and tell everybody the truth.

And don't have Ben try to stop me. I kind of like him."

"He won't stop you," said Morehouse. "Go on out and yell your head off. They've all been told you'll deny being tied up with me. We've whispered that you're being kept under cover until we're ready to spring you on Roberts. When a man invests his hard earned money, he likes to be in on little secrets like that. It makes everything seem more honest and above board when you trust the stockholders. Why they've even formed committees to follow you around so Roberts' toughs can't do us any harm. You say I'm not smart, huh?"

Gale smothered his anger. "All right, Spence," he said. "We part company here and now. Maybe you can think up something to tell your investors when your engineer turns up missing."

"I've already thought of it," said Morehouse, lazing back in his chair. "I'll tell them I was fooled, the same as they were. I'll tell them my engineer ran off with all the money."

Gale smashed his fist down on the table top. "Then I'll find the men who have paid in and give them their money back."

"No you won't," said Morehouse. "You don't know who they are and I won't tell you. And, if you're dumb enough to make a public announcement, this is what will happen. Half the town will show up, claiming they bought stock. You couldn't find enough gold in Stockton to pay them off, Ward. I know these boys."

Gale stood motionless and silent so long, Morehouse burst out laughing. "This time you're holding the bet while I have the fun. I've got it all thought out and there's nothing you can do about it."

Gale crowded against the table. Morehouse jumped up, backing away.

"Watch him, Ben."

The fat man shifted to free his guns, stopping as Gale laughed. "What's the matter, Spence?" said Gale. "You've got me. I'm in a box. I'll help you sell your stock."

He watched Morehouse relax, taking his time. "But you're planning to run out as soon as you have the money in your hand. You're not going to run, Spence. I'm going to make you build that water ditch. We'll give the miners such cheap water Roberts won't be able to sell a drop. I'm going to use you, Morehouse, the way you tried to use me. I'll use you and your ditch to break Matt Roberts. Now, damn you and your smart tricks, how do you like that?"

He saw real concern leap into Spencer's eyes, and behind him, Gale heard Derksen's sudden chuckle as the fat man said, "Why I guess he's got you, Spence. I guess maybe he's smarter than you are." And by the tone of the man's voice, Gale knew Derksen had changed sides. From now on the fat man belonged to him.

Gale watched Morehouse think about it. The small man said finally, "We'll see, Ward. We'll see. We're stuck in Stockton. How do you expect to get to Carolina? Walk?" He grinned and his good humor returned.

"We'll ride the stage," said Gale.

"Sure," said Morehouse. "I can just see Matt Roberts. He won't even charge us. He'd love to have us ride his stage."

Ben Derksen started to laugh. "Sure. I'll bet."

Gale turned to look at the fat man. "You afraid of Roberts, Ben?"

"I'm not afraid of anyone," Derksen was not bragging, but he had a certain pride. "But how are you going to get on the stage?"

"We'll steal a ride," said Gale.

"That's impossible," said Morehouse.

Derksen's small round eyes were thoughtful. "He licked Burns, Spence. Remember that. A man who can lick Burns can do almost anything if he wants to bad enough."

"I want to bad enough," said Gale. "I didn't travel six thousand miles to rot here in this Stockton mud."

3

In the morning, Ward Gale came out of the Stockton House and stepped onto the muddy sidewalk. He spread his feet apart and let the mire grip him. His big body broke the milling crowd and made a little eddy into which Spencer Morehouse moved his slighter build.

Morehouse was still bitter and protesting. Gale, not trusting him, carried the gold which the smaller man had collected.

Across the street, before the stage office, the high-wheeled mud wagon stood motionless. Glittering with red paint, its sides were decorated with gold lettering, "ROBERTS EXPRESS".

Against the drab mud and canvas and plank buildings the outfit looked fancy. Roberts new character showed in everything he owned. His boats were the newest and the best, his horses well cared for and spirited. His equipment always looked new and fresh painted to attract other men. How he used it was something else. Even the woman he had chosen, Gale thought, had been picked for her attractiveness.

The driver, chunky and motionless as he held the restless team in hand, was also spruce, for Roberts insisted that all his employees be well dressed and clean shaven. Gale watched the man.

"Who's driving?"

"Bill Conroy." Morehouse's tone was short. "This is a silly business. You'll get us all killed. Conroy's dangerous."

"I don't think so," said Gale, and shifted his attention to the crowd, knowing there must be several of Roberts' bruisers present. "If we have trouble, everyone who's invested in your water company will help us fight. They better."

Morehouse mumbled an answer which Gale failed to catch. Prudence Kellogg and her father had moved from the express office with Roberts behind them, trailed by the agent who carried the baggage and the mail.

Gale centered the full edge of his attention on Roberts, weighing his former friend, noting the man's proprietary interest in the girl, the way Roberts helped her into the rear seat and then stepped back while Kellogg hoisted his frail body to a place beside her. Then Roberts stepped into the center seat as the other passengers appeared in the office doorway.

Ben Derksen moved instantly from his position against the building front and cut these passengers off. Gale threw himself forward into the crowd, opening a path through the jammed street and came against his side of the mud wagon as Derksen's fat body moved against the other.

Seeing Derksen and guessing his intent, Bill Conroy raised

his whip, his voice a little shrill with concern. "Keep off, Ben. Keep off."

Roberts turned quickly to watch Derksen, and Gale swung into the wagon, followed by Morehouse. Gale reached and caught the tip of Conroy's back held whip. As Conroy turned, Derksen swung up, his weight making the braces creak.

Morehouse had his pepperbox in his small hand, covering Roberts. Now that the action had started, his black eyes glittered with excitement. Gale's gun was still in his belt. He left Roberts for Morehouse and Derksen. Sliding an arm around Conroy's neck, he shoved a fist into the man's throat, pulling his head back and half choking him.

With his other hand he seized the reins, shaking them loose. The team reared and the startled hostlers jumped for safety. Only now did the crowd realize what was happening as the horses lunged into their collars and bolted.

Men scurried out of their way, yelling. The red wheels spun, throwing off great clods of mud as they charged up Center Street, Gale fighting the team with one hand and trying to hold Conroy with the other. Not until they were clear of Stockton, did he release his grip on Conroy, shoving the lines back into the angry man's hands. Then he turned and smiled at Roberts.

"Sorry, Matt. We couldn't figure any other way to get to Carolina."

Prudence Kellogg had watched in amazement. Everything had happened so rapidly she had hardly had time to gasp. But her father did not bother to conceal his amusement. He hated Matt Roberts so thoroughly that it made him an automatic partisan of anyone who attacked the stage owner.

Roberts had not spoken. He sat, white-faced, careful under the threat of Morehouse's gun pressed against his ear. On his other side, Derksen's huge bulk overflowed, crowding him against Morehouse.

Gale ran his hands over Conroy and pulled a gun from the man's belt, sending it spinning into the mud. Using this as a signal, Morehouse did the same with Matt Roberts. Then his pepperbox disappeared into his pocket, and he stretched, well satisfied with himself.

"That, Ward," he said, "was a neat trick. I've heard of a stage being held up, but I never saw one stolen before."

Roberts ignored him. It was to Derksen that he spoke. "You're in bad company, Ben. I'll not forget this, or your part in it."

"Why," said Derksen, lazily, "I guess I'd feel real bad if you did forget it. I guess I don't like you much." He gave Roberts a childlike smile, then twisted, shoving an elbow into the man's side as he said to the girl, "How are you, Miss Prudence? You comfortable back there? We left in such a hurry. But you see we got a water company to build."

"Ben," said Prudence, and showed by her tone she had some liking for the fat man, "Mr. Roberts is right. You're in bad company. Both these men are swindlers. They have no intention, whatever, of building anything. All they mean to do is to sell stock to the miners and then disappear with the money."

Derksen shook his head. He was an open person with no reticence. "You're wrong," he said. "That's what Spence planned to do. But Gale won't let him run away. Gale's going to make him build that water ditch."

Prudence Kellogg was startled. "Why?" she asked.

Derksen used a hand to scratch the edge of his ear. "Well, now, I don't rightly know. He's never said, except that he hates Matt Roberts. Why are you going to build that water ditch, Mr. Gale?"

Morehouse was trying to shut Ben up, but Gale turned his head and met the girl's eyes upon him. Color came up quickly into her face and she looked away.

"Let's leave it at that, Ben," Gale told the fat man. "I hate Matt Roberts. I think I have good reasons for hating you, don't I, Matt?"

Roberts didn't answer.

"And a second water company in Carolina will certainly not help your business."

Roberts made an effort to hold his temper. "I said on the boat that I don't know you. I still don't, and I don't see the reason for your pretense."

He turned to the girl and her father. "I'm sorry that this happened to you on one of my stages. There is, of course, little or no law in this country."

Ben Derksen laughed. "You know, Matt, the trouble with you is that you're getting all-fired important. I remember when you first sailed into the bay. You sold your boat and cargo and you had some money, but you still wasn't nothing but a swab-headed sailor ashore. Now you really give yourself airs."

Roberts glared but said nothing. Prudence was watching him, her eyes puzzled as she thought. Why does Matt keep denying that he knows this man? It's obvious that he does, that there must be something bitter between them. She looked at Gale, unconcerned and apparently relaxed. Certainly if he were worried at bucking Matt Roberts he gave no sign. Who is he, she thought. I've got to find out.

4.

THE TEAM SLOWED FINALLY, their energies sucked out by the gripping mud. But their progress was faster than that of the ponderous freight wagons, mired so deeply that their axles dragged.

The road was fenced by discarded things, clothing and broken tools and wagon wheels, the flotsam of a hurried, uncaring migration that had streamed out wildly across this San Joaquin plain toward the illusive riches of the gold camps beyond.

The sun had come out and here and there patches of water glistened. Even the small hillocks were soaked. The whole country was little better than a morass and to Gale's brooding mind it was hard to conceive that any place in California men could actually need water enough to buy it.

Far to the east the green lift of the foothills broke the symmetry of the flat land. And beyond, rising from a purple haze, the higher peaks of the Sierra Nevadas with their everlasting snows, swam lace-like against the banked clouds.

In spite of the dull ache of his anger which had absorbed his full attention for months, Gale felt a stir of interest. This land was so vast, so unending.

Morehouse had talked long during the preceding night. This was the rainy season, unprecedented in its intensity. But once the rains had stopped, the foothills would soon turn dry and dusty and Carolina, sitting astraddle of its ancient river channel, would be a good five miles from water.

This, then, in other circumstances, could have offered a

real opportunity. A chance for a man to build something permanent. Something for profit, yet also for service. But riding in the jolting wagon, Ward Gale measured the opportunity against one thing only, its effect on Matt Roberts. He was not deceived by Roberts' quietness, by the man's apparent acceptance of the situation. He knew Roberts was worried and the thought pleased him. But he also knew he must be constantly on his guard. Roberts, having come this far and done this much, could not stop now. And only Ward Gale, out of all those in California, linked him with his past.

At six o'clock the tired horses dragged them into the rutted yard beside Simmons' Tent. Gale stepped down stiffly, staring at the huge canvas and board structure. This was something he had not counted on, stopping for the night. There were at least twenty men loafing about the entrance. He turned to Morehouse, and asked in an undertone, "Does this place belong to Roberts?"

The small man shrugged. "It's a stage stop. He's got some hostlers here. The tent belongs to Simmons. It's the halfway point." He turned his cocky grin up at Gale. "Looks like I better sell some stock so we have some friends in this crowd."

"You better spend your time watching the stage," said Gale.

"Let Ben do that," said Morehouse.

Derksen, who had joined them, complained. "Look, Spence. Always I'm the man who has to sleep out in the cold while you can go inside where the whisky is."

Morehouse said, angrily, "You didn't do such a good job in Stockton, Ben. We wouldn't be in this spot if you'd kept your eyes open there. No whisky for you until we get to Carolina."

"One little drink?" Derksen appealed to Gale. "A man gets powerful dry riding through mud all day."

Gale said, "One drink, but I'll bring it to you. Get back on that stage and watch Conroy every minute. That's an order."

Wilson Kellogg helped his daughter from the stage. Morehouse, with ready courtesy, came forward and took the girl's bags and the three of them made a small group on their way toward the Tent.

The stage pulled on toward the corral, Conroy driving, Derksen's bulk on the seat at his side. And, for the first time in years, Gale found himself alone with Matt Roberts.

Roberts waited until the Kelloggs had disappeared inside before he spoke. Then he said, in a toneless voice, "You won't get away with this, Ward. Everything's stacked against you. I own this country."

"I owned a ship, once," said Gale.

"What ship?" said Roberts. "My papers were in order when I sailed the Witch into San Francisco. Who would believe you against me?"

"You killed Peter."

"Did I? That's a serious charge you're making, Ward. Could you prove it?"

"I'm not going to try," said Gale. "I came here to kill you, but now I've changed my mind. Instead of that I'm going to strip you of everything you own and everything you want, until you have nothing at all. Then, maybe, I'll kill you."

Roberts did not seem impressed. "You think so, Ward? Why you damned fool, I could stop you right here. But I'm going to let you come on to Carolina. When you get there, the Kelloggs won't be with you every night. Remember that." He turned away then and moved toward the Tent, careful where he stepped so that the mud would not soil his glistening boots.

Watching him go Gale realized Roberts had changed. This man was not the same as the one who had sailed out of Boston two years before. The arrogance of success, and confidence in the methods he had used to attain it, had armored Roberts against all uncertainty. A feeling of futility came to Gale and he wondered if he had not been a fool to listen to Morehouse. His own way would have been much simpler. He could do it now and not worry about traveling further. But he could not do it now.

He called after Roberts, "The Kelloggs won't be with you every night, either, Matt."

Supper finished, Gale loafed in the Tent and considered the long room, through the eddying smoke of his cigar. The building was divided into unequal parts by a canvas wall, the smaller portion reserved for women travelers. The larger section was one room, unfurnished save for a plank bar at one end with its whisky keg.

Men were already rolled in their blankets, sleeping on the packed earth of the floor. Morehouse stood beside the bar talking eagerly to some prospective stock buyers. Neither Roberts nor Kellogg was in sight.

Made restless by their absence and remembering Derksen's drink, Gale moved to the bar, filled one of the tin cups half up with the fiery liquor and stepped out into the night.

It was still clear. The dark arch of the sky was speckled to almost a milky whiteness by a myriad of stars. The night wind had lost its chill and came soft from the distant hills.

Gale stood a moment, letting his eye pupils contract after the glare of the sputtering lamps. Then, when he picked up his night sight, he moved toward the corral, alert to everything around him. To the right, beyond the corral fence, a fire flickered up into the darkness. Around this blaze huddled a dozen Californianos, their voices rising softly, yet mournfully, in a Spanish song.

He paused to listen, wondering how these men felt, their homeland invaded by a horde of foreigners. Then he moved on toward the corral.

Inside the pole structure the horses moved restlessly, chomping at the few spears of grass around the edges of the barrier. The stage made a high, dark outline, and heading for this he heard the click of a cocking gun and stopped motionless. Ben Derksen's heavy voice reached him. "Speak out. Who are you?"

"Ah," said Gale. "So you're still awake?" and continued forward. "I brought your drink."

Ben seized the cup and drained it before he answered. "Why thanks," he said, then. "After what you said I guessed one drink would be all I'd get."

"Who gave you the other one?"

"Why Spence did," said Derksen, with great satisfaction. "He brought it when he brought my supper."

Gale relaxed, "Have you seen Roberts?"

Derksen said, shrewdly, "You thought maybe Roberts was feeding me liquor, huh? You know, Mr. Gale, you're worrying about Roberts. I guessed the idea was for you to worry him."

"That's the idea," said Gale.

"When a man gets spooky," said Ben, smacking his lips, "he's liable to miss what he aims at. A spooky man don't think clear."

"That's right, Ben."

"You bet. So you got to keep crowding Roberts. You worried him when you licked Burns. You worried him when you stole the stage. It worried him when I told him about the water ditch. But he ain't spooked yet. You'll have to keep pushing him all the time until he gets spooky. Then I guess he'll make a mistake. How you going to push him tonight?"

"Here?" said Gale. "I don't know."

"You got to think up a way, Mr. Gale. You can't let him rest quiet for a minute. Not Matt, you can't."

Gale did not answer. He swung away from the stage and slowly circled the corral. He took no stock in Roberts' word that the man would let them proceed to Carolina. Roberts' and Conroy's disappearance bothered him and each shadow held a danger now.

At the corner of the fence nearest the fire, he stopped, still in shadow, and searched the group about the flame. Neither Roberts nor Conroy was there. There was no chance of error here. The dress of these men was foreign as the voices which still rose in song. Firelight warmed their silver ornaments and, back of them, the blaze flickered softly on the crucifix of a black-robed priest.

The melody of the song reached into Gale, loosening the tightness that had grown on him. He leaned back against the fence, letting the music flow through him. When he heard the step he whirled. Someone came toward him along the dark fence. He loosened his gun and said, "That's close enough."

The figure stopped. Then Wilson Kellogg spoke clearly. "It's me, sir. I've been looking for you."

"All right," said Gale and moved into the deeper shadows toward the man. "What do you want?"

"To talk to you," said Kellogg. "There are some things, sir, I want to understand."

"What?" said Gale.

"Your attitude toward Roberts."

"That," said Gale, "is my business."

"No," said Kellogg. "It may affect us all. Are you honestly intending to build this water ditch?"

"I'm going to build it," said Gale.

"Why, sir? Because you want the ditch, or because you hate Matt Roberts?"

"What difference does that make to you or anyone else?"

"It makes no difference to me," said Kellogg, slowly, "as long as you build the ditch. But it could make a big difference to you. There's something between you and Matt Roberts. I take no stock in his denial that he knows you. I, sir, hold myself a good judge of men."

"Then," said Gale, "keep away from me."

"No," said Kellogg. "You're hard and bitter but it will take a hard man to complete that water ditch. You'll need help. I have come to offer you what help I can give."

Gale looked at him half curiously. "You hate Roberts, too," he said.

"That isn't important," said Kellogg. "I love Carolina. I have great dreams for the town. I am trying to have it made the state capital. That's why I'll help you with this second water ditch, if you will accept me, sir."

Gale stuck out his hand. Kellogg's grip was firm and warm. "Thank you, Mr. Gale," said Kellogg, and walked away.

3

Prudence Kellogg came swiftly out of the darkness a moment after her father had turned the corner of the corral. She stopped before Gale, standing straight and stiff and angry.

"What were you talking to my father about?"

Gale was surprised to see her. All during the ride from Stockton to Simmons' Tent he had found himself disquieted by her presence, but he had been forced to watch Matt Roberts, to be constantly on his guard against a possible attack by Conroy.

But now, standing in the deep darkness he had the time to consider her, to remember with sharp clearness the action in the boat cabin, to recall how warm her lips had been against his, how firm her body.

He smiled a little. It was one of the few pleasant memories of the trip, and yet a thought crossed his mind to cloud it. She belonged to Matt Roberts. She was promised in marriage to the man whom he had planned to kill.

Looking at her he found that he was puzzled. How could a girl like this give herself to Roberts? Was she blinded by the man's success, by his personality? Did she actually love him?

As soon as the thought came his smile widened a little. It would be amusing to find out. It would be amusing to pit himself against Roberts. Why not? He had set himself to ruin Roberts, to strip him of everything that he wished, and certainly Roberts wanted this girl far more than he wanted the other things he held. If he could take Prudence and do with her as he wished it might drive Roberts to fury. At least it would be worth trying, and the girl was worth the try. He had never met anyone who quickened his blood the way she did.

But first he needed to win her confidence, and to destroy her trust in Roberts, and he set himself the task as deliberately as if he were planning a campaign.

"You were close enough to hear what was said," he told her. "Why pretend that you did not overhear? Be honest with me. I have tried to be honest with you."

She flushed.

"And about the night on the boat," he added. "I could tell you that I was sorry, but I would not be honest then, for I am not. It was one of the great experiences of my life. I won't forget it, I'll treasure the feel of your lips on mine for as long as I live."

Prudence Kellogg gasped. This man never said what she

expected, nor reacted as she expected. She had had to admit to herself in the privacy of her cabin that he had stirred her more than any man she had ever known. And she felt now a quick sense of pleasure at his words, but she crowded it away from her, managing to say coldly,

"You talk about honesty. I don't believe that you even know the meaning of the word. I think that you are worse than Spencer Morehouse. My father is gullible. He wants to help the town, and the people in it, and he will listen to almost anyone who offers him a way of accomplishing what he wants. But I'm not gullible, Mr. Gale. I know that it takes more than words to make honesty."

He stepped closer to her, so that she was forced to look up a little into his face. "Listen to me, Prudence. You are the one who is blind to honesty. You've promised youself to Matt Roberts, and what I do threatens Roberts, so you are willing to believe the worst of me."

"That's not true. I . . ."

"Tell me one thing that I have done," Gale said, "to make you believe that I am imposing on your father? I know that Morehouse has a bad reputation. You've told me so, and I am certainly not defending him, but look at it for one moment from my angle. Morehouse put into my head the idea of building this water company. It interests me, but I am unknown in Carolina.

"But your father is well known, and respected. If I am going to accomplish what I have set out to do, I need someone like him to front for my water company. Since he too desires to have another ditch built, why should I not join forces with him?"

"So that he can front for your swindle . . ."

He took both her shoulders between his big hands. She tried to pull away, to fight against the magnetism of his body, but he held her easily. "Wait a minute, I haven't finished. This is not a swindle. We are going to build that ditch . . ."

"But only because you hate Matt Roberts . . ."

"You," he said, "are all mixed up. Of course I hate Roberts. I have never denied it. The very fact that I do hate him should make you realize that I am going to build that ditch. Use your head. Would it hurt Roberts if I helped

Morehouse swindle the miners by collecting money and then running out without building the water company? Of course it wouldn't. I've got to build the second ditch in order to ruin Roberts' business."

Unwillingly she was more than half convinced. "But if you are honest, why involve yourself with Morehouse?"

"Why not, as long as I can twist him to my own purposes? I'll use Morehouse, or your father, or even you to strike at Roberts, to pull him down, to grind, to squeeze the life out of him."

"Me?"

Gale took a deep breath. He had not intended to say that. He had allowed his hatred of Roberts to carry him away for a moment, but it was not too late to repair the damage. In fact it might be handled better that way. If he was apparently honest, if he seemed to be putting all his cards on the table it might help to break down her reserve.

"You," he said. "Which do you think means the most to Matt Roberts, you or his water company?"

She gasped a little. "Really, Mr. Gale, I never knew anyone quite like you."

"No," he told her. "You didn't. I see something, I want it, and I go after it."

Her laugh was a little shaky. "Meaning me?" She tried to say it lightly, but somehow failed.

"Meaning you." His tone had softened a little. "I had been months at sea, and suddenly I saw a beautiful woman in a cabin. I held her in my arms, and kissed her, and her robe fell open . . ." It was too dark for Gale to see her face clearly but he guessed that it was crimson. He felt her arms stiffen under his grasp, but she said nothing.

"A beautiful woman," he continued. "I went back on deck and dreamed a dream as any man might, and then I find that she had promised herself to a thief like Roberts, a thief and a murderer."

She tried again to pull free. "You are crazy. Captain Roberts a thief . . . a murderer . . ."

For an instant Gale started to tell her about his ship, about his dead brother, but he had no proof, no means of convincing her, and then he thought of something else. He spoke without considering, never guessing that he might regret the hasty words in the near future.

"And then I thought that I was worried needlessly, for you can't marry Matt Roberts."

"I can't?" She laughed almost brazenly. "We'll see about that, Mr. Gale. I fully intend to marry him."

"No," said Gale. "You can't, legally, not while his wife still lives in Boston, caring for the children he deserted."

She gasped, but Gale went on. Now that he had started his lie it was easy to continue. "Three children. A man's past finally catches up with him. I wouldn't stand aside and let that happen to you."

She was staring at him. "How . . . I . . . how can I believe you?"

He shrugged. "Roberts has denied knowing me. Ask yourself why he should since it's obvious that I know him. He denied it for fear of what I might tell you, for fear that you might believe me." He watched her closely. If he knew anything about women this should get her. A woman might condone stealing, or even killing, but she would never condone a tie to another woman.

She was still staring up at him and he let her go, and watched her as the cold anger grew in her. "How could he?"

"Why not," said Gale. "He is three thousand miles from home. The communications are bad. Even if you found him out later he would have had you. Roberts tires of things easily."

The darkness hid her angry flush. "Yes, that's what I thought," she was speaking to herself. "Ever since he came to Carolina I've watched him. He can be ruthless, but he can also seem kind and generous and strong."

Gale had sense enough to remain quiet.

"I thought I could marry him." She was still speaking to herself. "I thought that I could change him, that I would have a home, security . . ." Suddenly she was crying. "What do you think of me? I was ready to marry a man I did not love because I thought it wise."

Gale's arms went around her. "Easy." Her head was pressed against his shoulder. "It's all right, you're through with Roberts. You don't need him any more. Hold on to me, let me help you."

She pulled away to look at him. "You mean that you want to marry me, after what I've just told you?"

He was startled. Ward Gale had known several women intimately during his life, but he had never seriously contemplated marriage. And then he thought, Why not? She's attractive. She touches me more than any woman ever has. I'm not in love with her, but if I should marry her, snatching her as it were from Roberts I would have won a good part of my battle against him.

He stooped then and kissed her. For an instant she was unresponsive, and then it was as if his nearness had awakened some latent spark within her and she came alive, her arm slipping around his neck, holding him tight, her body straining against him fiercely.

Finally she broke away, shivering. "This is crazy."

It was crazy, but at the instant Gale was not thinking clearly.

"We hardly know each other."

"Don't we?" he said. "I venture that I saw more of you the other night than any man has ever seen. What more is there to know, if you think you want me?"

She was too honest to quibble. "I do . . . oh . . . I do." She came back into his arms. "I know that this can't last, that it makes no sense at all."

"Life makes very little sense. Are you afraid?"

"Not of you. Never of you, my darling."

He looked around. He was thinking quickly. I've got to keep her from talking to Roberts in the morning. I've got to prevent him from denying my impossible story until this is over. I've . . . and then his eyes fell on the priest beside the fire and the thought leaped into his head.

"Marry me tonight."

"Tonight?"

"Now. There is a priest, over by the fire. This is a new country, Prudence, and a wild one. Who knows what tomorrow will bring? Marry me tonight."

She pushed back, holding both her small hands on his shoulders, trying to study his face, trying to read it in the darkness. "All right," she said. "All right, Ward Gale." He tried to kiss her but she turned her head aside.

"Not yet." She took his hand then and led him toward the camp fire.

The priest had little English, but he was a kindly man. He read the sparks in the girl's eyes, and talked of the rules of the church he served and the banns which should be published, and then he looked again at Prudence's eyes and forgot them.

By the light of the dancing fire, with the respectful Californians grouped around them, he read the holy service, softly, in his own language.

Neither Gale nor Prudence understood the words, but no one listening to the intonations of his mellow voice could doubt the seriousness with which he viewed the occasion.

Then it was finished, and Gale found himself smiling and shaking hands with men, strangers all, whom he would probably never meet again. Yet he felt a warm kinship for them at the moment which lingered long after he had retreated from the fire light.

They walked away together, the girl clinging to his arm. She was muted with embarrassment now, seeming to have lost her certainness now that the event was passed.

"Ward."

He bent close to her.

"It's terrible," she told him in a small voice. "Our wedding night, and no place that we can go to be alone."

His blood quickened, for he had not thought of that. "Alone," he swept his arm in a wide gesture, indicating the far reaching, rolling ground. "We have a thousand square leagues to be alone in, Mrs. Gale."

She caught her breath at his words. "Out here, like . . . like some Indian woman?"

He laughed then. He could not help it, though the sound was gentle. "Indian women suffer from the same impulses, the same longings as you do. Will a roof change things, would a roof give us more privacy?"

She did not protest again. They continued on until they found a quiet, sheltered place and sitting down his questing fingers fumbled with the fastenings of her dress.

"Ward, please, wait. I'm afraid . . ."

"Of what? What is there to fear?"

"I don't know."

He had the fastenings undone. Gently he let his hands run
up over the warm softness of her skin and felt her shiver
beneath his touch, and then suddenly her hands were reaching for him, dragging him down, pressing him against her
as she gave herself fully and awkwardly to him, crying a
little as she did so, crying from the full realization of her
happiness.

Afterwards they lay in each other's arms, staring upward
at the distant stars, not speaking, each too filled with his
own thoughts for words.

4

Later, after Gale had returned her to the Tent and walked
into the men's quarters after bidding her good night he saw
Roberts and Conroy stretched out side by side, sleeping. He
had an impulse to rouse Roberts and tell him of the marriage, and to laugh at the blank anger which he knew would
show in the man's face. But he crowded down the impulse
and turned away, still wanting to talk, still with the need
to tell someone.

The lamps had been turned low and the floor was well
covered with blanketed figures. He had difficulty in locating
Morehouse, but when he did find him, the little man sat up
instantly, wide awake. Gale motioned toward the door.

Morehouse, suspecting trouble, freed his pepperbox and
came quickly to his feet, threading his way between the
sleepers with the lightness of a cat.

Gale went on ten long paces from the Tent before he
stopped. Morehouse closed up behind him, whispering ur-
gently, "What's the matter? What's happened?"

"I'm married," said Gale.

"What of it?" said Morehouse. "The world's full of crazy
people. Does that change our plans?"

"I was married tonight," said Gale. "I married Prudence
Kellogg."

The little man's jaw went slack. "You what?"

"I married Prudence Kellogg," said Gale.

"But why?" said Morehouse, not whispering now. "You
don't know her. You can't love her. Why did you do it?"

"She was going to marry Matt Roberts," said Gale. "I couldn't let her do that."

"So that's it." Morehouse was genuinely shocked. "My God, Ward, do you realize what you've done?"

"I know exactly what I've done," said Gale.

"So do I," said Morehouse. "And I've never heard of a lower piece of business, dragging a woman into your fight with Roberts. I should have let you kill him."

"Wait," said Gale. "You're the one who told me to be hard headed. To use any means at hand."

"But not this," said Morehouse, strangely agitated. "In this country, Ward, women are something special. There aren't many. Every man in California would turn against you if they learned what you've done tonight. For your own private revenge, to drag a woman into this."

"Look who's talking," said Gale. "You bragged that you had no ethics."

"I haven't," said Morehouse. "I don't even like the girl for the way she's interfered with me. But I respect her as a woman. If I were half the man I ought to be, I'd call you out."

"Listen to me," said Gale. "She was going to marry Roberts. She didn't love him. She admitted it. But she was going to marry him. Think who he is. A murderer. A thief."

"Don't try to justify yourself to me," said Morehouse.

"I don't care what you think, Spence," said Gale. "I'm doing what I have to do. I'll only tell you this. Prudence will never be hurt through any act of mine. Whatever my motives, she's better off married to me than to Matt Roberts."

Morehouse made an impatient motion with his hands and started for the Tent. Before he had gone a half dozen steps, he turned slowly back. "Ward," he said, thoughtfully, "how did you do it? How did you make her change her mind?"

"I told her," said Gale, "that Roberts had a wife and children in Boston."

"Oh," said Morehouse. "Why didn't you say so? I didn't know that."

"Neither did I," said Gale. "But I couldn't let her marry Roberts."

Morehouse looked at him for a long time. Then he slowly shook his head. "Ward, my friend, you've bought yourself an awful lot of trouble tonight. I wouldn't be in your shoes for all the money in Carolina."

5.

Thinking a lot, Gale slept little. At daybreak, with men beginning to stir, he rose and made his way to the corral. Derksen still slept heavily, his big body wrapped in his blanket coat, huddled against the stage wheel.

Gale nudged him awake and Derksen was instantly on his feet. "Oh," said Ben. "It's you."

"Go get some breakfast," said Gale. "I'll see Conroy doesn't leave without us."

He leaned idly against the fence, watching the hostlers feed the teams. Conroy moved sleepily toward him, made surly and ill-humored by the stinging cold of the morning air. He passed Gale without a word and entered the corral to supervise the harnessing.

Kellogg stepped into the morning sun, turning toward the women's entrance, and Gale watched him closely until he disappeared. A few minutes later, Kellogg came out. The older man was hurrying now, moving more rapidly than Gale had ever seen him.

Suddenly Kellogg stopped, as if he looked for a direction for his haste. Then seeing Gale he came quickly toward the stage.

Gale said, "Good morning," in a neutral tone.

"Ward," said the older man, "I want to talk to you."

"Of course," said Gale. "I expected you to."

"Why did you do it?" said Kellogg.

"Didn't Prudence tell you that?"

"Prudence told me her side. I want yours. I want the truth. I told you last night that I'm a fair judge of men. I told you last night that I thought you were hard and bitter enough to fight Matt Roberts. What's between you and Roberts?"

"Does that matter?"

"It can be very important now." Wilson Kellogg was obviously holding himself in, wanting to be fair. "There's something very serious between you and Roberts. Prudence is my daughter. I think I have a right to know the truth."

Gale breathed deeply. "All right," he said. He told Kellogg, never raising his voice. "When this sailor came back to Boston and told me what had happened, I traveled all the way to California to kill Matt Roberts."

"What are you waiting for?" asked Kellogg.

"Because," said Gale. "I have a better idea now."

"I see," said Kellogg. "There could only be one better way; to take from Roberts everything he wants. He wanted Prudence."

"Wait," said Gale.

"You wait," said Kellogg, his frail body straightening. "I don't know why, but she loves you, Ward. I don't know whether you love her or not. I'm not going to ask you. You could lie too easily about that. But if you hurt her, Ward, if you bring her any grief, I'll kill you."

"If I hurt her," said Gale, woodenly, "if I bring her any grief, you do that. I won't try to stop you."

He broke off as the teams were led from the corral and, turning, walked toward the Tent.

When Conroy drove the teams up, Ben Derksen appeared picking his teeth and blinking into the sun. Morehouse, behind him, hung back. Prudence came from the women's side, carrying her luggage. Gale took it from her and she squeezed his hand. "Good morning, Mr. Gale," she said, making the name ring. Her face was flushed, her eyes dancing.

Gale smiled at her, murmuring his greeting. He carried the baggage to the rear boot and, opening the flap, stowed it within. At that moment, Roberts came through the door, shouldering Morehouse out of his way, and smiled at Prudence.

"I'll ride with you from here on, my dear," he said, and offered his hand to help her up.

Gale straightened, letting the boot lid drop. "No, Matt," he said, walking up. "I'll ride with my wife. You'll forgive me if I act like a jealous husband."

Roberts half turned, then was suddenly very still. His handsome face tightened and turned grey. "What did you say?"

Gale said, blandly, "Why haven't you heard? Prudence and I were married last night."

The thinly clothed violence in Roberts broke through. Wildness showed in his eyes and he came suddenly at Gale, charging. But Derksen, even though caught flatfooted with surprise, proved what Morehouse had said. He threw his big body at Roberts, driving him over against the stage wheel and lifting his shoulder under Roberts' chin, pinned him there. At the same time he dropped his other hand to his gun and looked at Conroy.

"Let him go!" said Gale. "Let him go!"

"No," said Prudence. "Please, Ward."

Behind them, Morehouse said, "Forget it, Ward. Forget it. Don't make it any worse than it is."

"Let him go, Ben," said Gale, in a slower, softer voice. "There'll be no trouble unless he makes it."

Derksen spoke to Roberts. "You feel better now, Matt?"

Roberts moved Ben two feet away with a quick shove. But that was all. He straightened his coat and faced Prudence. "Why did you do it?" he said.

"I know about you, Matt," she told him hotly. "I found out."

"From Gale? And you believed him?"

"I'll always believe him," she said, and smiled up at Gale.

Saying no more, Roberts turned away and took the place beside Bill Conroy. The rest of them climbed in.

2

Carolina was two years old. Of all the camps in the southern mines, it most resembled an eastern town. Many of the camps were built in twisting, narrow gulches, but Carolina had room to grow and its earliest citizens had come from New England, bringing with them the idea of a town common.

The Square remained, flanked on the east by Washington Street, which had developed into the main thoroughfare. On the west, the boundary was Adams, while north and south, Gold and Silver edged it respectively.

Grouped on these four streets, facing the Square, were the solid businesses of the community: The Union Exchange Hotel and the Holbrook House; Roberts Express and Bank; and Emil Aruup's Trading Company.

Along Washington were the saloons and gambling places. Behind them in a jumbled mass of twisting alleys and dusty courts, lay the Concho, mud-walled and dirty, its denizens never crossing Washington into the better part of town.

The Concho district was Darlington's. His was the biggest saloon, the biggest gambling house. From this place his weight was felt in every crooked alley and cluttered court.

Each sundown he stood in the alley beside his place. Standing there, the sun at his back threw his long shadow across Washington and more respectable men had to walk over it. This, somehow, pleased him.

He was a tall and dark man, thin and sardonic, a man who knew the secrets of this town. He banked these secrets in his mind and let them earn interest against the day he would have to draw on the account.

He saw the stage wheel into Gold and draw up before the Express Office, and almost ignored it. Then the grouping of the passengers caught his full attention and brought him alert: Roberts riding at Conroy's side, Prudence Kellogg occupying the rear seat between her father and a stranger, while Ben Derksen and Spencer Morehouse held the center place.

Darlington stood motionless and watched Roberts step down with never a backward glance and disappear into the Bank beside the Express Office. He watched the stranger help Prudence to the ground, gather up the luggage, pause for a moment to speak to Derksen and Morehouse. Then the group separated, the stranger cutting across the Square with the Kelloggs. They passed the Hangman's Oak, the lone tree in the middle of the Square, and disappeared up Adams.

Morehouse and Derksen came diagonally toward Darlington. But instead of crossing Washington they swung to cross Silver and enter Holbrook House. Not until they had gone did Darlington stir. Then he lighted one of his crooked cheroots and turned to enter the side door of the saloon.

His sister Cherry stood in the doorway, watching him. Blonde as he was dark, she made a striking figure in her red dress and he had the momentary conviction that there was not a better looking woman in California. He thought, If I had chosen to be a gentleman, she could have been a queen.

She smiled as he came up. "What interests you tonight, Phil?"

He was evasive from habit. "What makes you think I was interested in anything?"

"Phil," she said, showing him a tenderness no one else had ever seen, "don't talk that way to me. You never stand out there after the sun has gone unless you're interested. What was it?"

"Roberts came in on the stage," he said. His secretiveness made it hard for him to talk freely, so Cherry kept waiting him out. "Prudence Kellogg came in too. They were in different seats. There was a stranger with her. Morehouse rode the stage, too. Morehouse riding in one of Roberts' wagons." He turned the words over slowly with his mind. "That doesn't make sense."

"Come in out of the night air," said Cherry. "You'll find out about it."

Darlington paused just inside the door, letting his eyes stray from one end of the long room to the other. This was his. From the front windows, with their colored, leaded panes along the lengthy, glistening bar with its expensive mirrors, to the gambling room at the rear, this was his. Carolina was the richest square mile on earth. But no claim, along its dry gulches, turned out one half the gold that passed across his bar and gaming tables.

As always, he made a slow circuit of the place, Cherry walking beside him. He checked the liquor stocks, inspected the glasses, then tasted a sliver of each of the meats, tasting the turkey twice. Satisfied, he moved on to the rear tables where the percentage girls loafed before their evening's work. Each one rose and pivoted slowly before him. When he was satisfied, he turned away from Cherry without a word and took his accustomed place at the end of the long bar. He was ready for the night.

A few customers straggled in, pausing for their first drink at the dark counter. Then the door opened and Ben Derksen came through. Unembarrassed, the fat man lifted a handful of sliced turkey on the way by and came on back. Pausing at Darlington's side, he spoke with his mouth full of meat. "Hello, Phil. How'd you like to invest in a water company?"

Darlington knew Derksen was not speaking to him alone. The fat man's voice was pitched too loud. And it had its effect. The growing noise in the room ceased.

"What water company?" said Darlington.

"The Miner's Mutual Water Company," said Ben. "Wilson Kellogg, president." He chuckled and dropped his pretense of talking to Darlington alone and turned to face the room. "See Spencer Morehouse about stock. And you better hurry, boys. We sold a lot of shares in Stockton."

Darlington asked, softly, "Does Roberts know?"

Derksen lowered his voice. "He knows all right."

Darlington motioned up a bartender. "What will you have, Ben?"

"Why," said Ben, "I don't care if I do and make it double rye. What was it-you wanted to know, Phil?"

The muscles at the corners of Darlington's eyes tightened a little. It had always annoyed him that Derksen, outwardly a simpleton, saw through almost every man's mask.

"Who was the stranger on the stage, Ben?"

"Him?" said Derksen, and emptied his glass. "He's an engineer, I guess. Come to build a water company. He's a man to watch, Phil. He licked Chauncey Burns in Stockton."

"He did?" Darlington did not try to hide his surprise.

"And that ain't all," said Ben, warming up. "He married Prudence Kellogg at Simmons' Tent."

3

Prudence waited until her father had disappeared into the parlor, then she said, "We're home, darling," and walked across the room into Gale's arms.

He held her close instinctively, stroking her hair, but his mind was on other things. This, he thought, is Roberts' town. I've bested him on the river boat, and in Stockton, and at the Tent. But what about here?

He had seen the way that men of this country reacted at Matt Roberts' name, and he realized the power which his former friend had attained and a small bell of warning sounded in his brain.

I'll be careful, he thought. I'll watch my every step. And then he realized that Prudence was speaking and brought his attention back to her.

"You aren't listening," she said. "You're acting like a true husband already. Come on, I'll show you the house."

He nodded and picking up the baggage followed her up the narrow stairway to the two rooms above. "That one," she said, nodding toward the right hand door at the head of the landing, "is father's. This is ours."

The room into which they stepped was obviously a woman's. The bed was a four poster with a canopy of flowered chintz. The curtains matched.

He looked around, feeling alien and out of place and slightly embarrassed. It was as if a woman had opened herself fully, suddenly, and exposed her innermost thoughts, her likes, and her inhibitions.

It had been different at the Tent. There they had been blanketed only by the sky, sheltered only by the small hillock which broke the wind. They had been sharing something without even truly knowing each other. He thought, Prudence is a complete stranger to me for all that I am married to her, for all that we have lain together.

He had an insane desire to turn and run. He felt trapped. He stood listening as she chattered while she unpacked. He thought, she accepts the situation much more realistically than I do. She feels married. She is married. I'm not. It's a crazy thing that I've done, trapping myself, binding myself to a woman whom I do not know.

At the moment he did not even feel any physical desire for her, although his eyes told him how beautiful she was. He heard her say,

"We'll need a bigger house, after we get settled, or perhaps you and I can keep this one after father goes to the State Senate."

"Oh," he said, only half following her words.

She laughed. "Of course if Carolina is chosen the capital, why then father will still be here."

"Will it be?"

She moved her shoulders. "Who knows what the legislature will do? Father and the men with him have worked very hard. They have the petitions signed, almost forty thousand names. They are downstairs now, and the legislature will find it hard to refuse. After all, this is the largest gold camp on the Mother Lode, and California's whole economy is based on gold.

"Benecia is not a good place. The town is built on a swamp, and when the capital was set up we knew it was only temporary. And as for the talk of Sacramento City, what has Sacramento to offer that we haven't?"

Gale did not know. He realized that this to him was an alien land, that its problems, its factions and its arguments touched him not at all, but he looked at her curiously, surprised by the emotion in her voice.

"This town seems to mean a great deal to you?"

"It means a great deal to my father," she corrected him. "All his life he has struggled for what he believed in, and everything he touched has turned to failure. This is his last chance. He's an old man. Help him, Gale. Help him for me."

She came against him then. She had been unbuttoning her dress as she talked, meaning to change, and it slipped down exposing one shoulder and the round swell of her breast.

"You will help?" She raised her face for his kiss and he obeyed dutifully, feeling suddenly that he had to get out of the room, away from there, someplace where he could think.

"Of course I'll help," he said. "I'll go and talk to your father now, while you are changing." He turned then and almost bolted through the door and rushed down the stairs, trying to control his emotions before he was called upon to face the older man. He paused in the hallway, looking in through the half open door and had a moment's feeling of relief. Kellogg was not there.

He moved through the door slowly, hesitantly. This was the room of another man, a man as much a stranger to him as was the girl he had left upstairs. He looked around, noting the writing table with its pens and ink, the ordered library, the books neat upon their shelves and in the far corner the stacks of the folded petitions.

He crossed to look down at them, and realized how much Kellogg had already done for his beloved town. He was still staring at them when Prudence spoke from the doorway behind him.

"You see what I was talking about. He has been circulating those for six months."

Gale turned, nodding. "I don't see how he can fail."

She looked around the room. "Where is he?"

Gale shook his head. "I don't know. He was gone when I first came down."

A shadow darkened her eyes, and he sensed suddenly that she was afraid. "I wish he hadn't gone out."

"He'll be back," said Gale, thinking that he knew what made her afraid.

"Of course," she gave him a quick smile. "Sit down, rest, while I get supper." She turned and vanished into the kitchen and Gale sat down. Half nervously he fumbled for a cigar, and not finding one in his pocket, opened Kellogg's humidor.

He lit it, strolling back into the hall and hesitated, then just as he was about to move into the kitchen, he heard the front door open and turned, expecting to see Kellogg. Instead Morehouse slipped through, halting at sight of Gale and saying in a relieved voice, "Oh, there you are. It isn't my fault."

Gale was startled. "What?"

"Kellogg," said Morehouse. "He's on the front steps. He's ashamed to come in."

Gale brushed past the little man and stepped out onto the porch. He saw Wilson Kellogg sitting on the steps, his back against one of the posts, his head bent forward, resting in his hands.

"Wilson," said Gale and moved to his side. "What is it, man, get up."

Kellogg rose with exaggerated dignity, putting one hand against the post to steady himself. "I tell you, sir," he said, "Matt Roberts is a dog. A despicable, yellow dog."

. Prudence pushed Morehouse aside and came up against Gale's arm. "Father!" she said.

"It's all right, my dear," said Kellogg. "It's quite all right." He started a weaving path toward the front door.

"Help him," Prudence ordered Gale.

Gale scooped the man up in his arms. "I'll take care of him," he said, and carried him up the stairs.

When he came back down again, Morehouse was still there, pacing back and forth across the parlor, Prudence watching him silently.

"All right, Spence," said Gale. "What was it this time?"

"We're all through," said Morehouse, and made no effort to keep the bitter tone from his voice. "We're through before we ever got started. Roberts moved too fast for us."

"What did he do?"

"He cut his water rates. I expected him to do that, but I thought he would wait a week or two until he was certain whether or not we were really a serious threat. I meant to move fast. I meant to get as much of the stock sold as I could." He broke off and looked at Gale, accusingly. "But you had to stir him up too much."

Gale said, "I wasn't asking about Roberts. What happened to Wilson?"

"There's nothing important about that," said Morehouse. "But he was in Darlington's. We both were, Roberts had men all over town circulating the news of the cut water rates. We went to Darlington's to try and talk it down. It was Darlington who got Wilson started. He does that when he wants a man to talk or to shut him up."

"So this is the end of your fine scheme," said Gale. "It didn't get very far, did it?"

Prudence looked from one to the other, incredulous. "You mean you're going to stop merely because Matt cut his water rates? Anyone would know he would do that."

Morehouse said, impatiently, "What else can we do? You know the miners as well as I do. They're gamblers. They live from day to day. Do you think anyone would invest in another water company when Roberts is going to sell water as cheaply as we can?"

"But it won't last," said Prudence. "You know he'll raise his rates again."

"Sure," said Morehouse. "But he won't raise his rates until we're done and gone from here. Don't you see what this means, Prudence? We have to get out of here." A faint sneer twisted his lips. "You know Matt."

She looked at Gale. "Are you afraid of Roberts, Ward?"

"No," said Gale.

"Then fight him," she said, fiercely. "Call the miners together. Have a meeting. I have more faith in their common sense than Mr. Morehouse does. At least make the effort. At least don't run."

"I have no intention of running," said Gale. "I don't know what good a miners' meeting will do, but we'll try it. We'll try anything. But I'll tell you this, as long as Matt Roberts is in Carolina, I'll be here, too."

"Here, maybe," said Morehouse. "But will you ever go out onto the street at night?"

Gale looked at him. "Arrange for the miners' meeting, Spence. Now, tell me where to find this Darlington."

Prudence caught his arm. "What about Darlington? What are you going to do?"

"Talk to him," said Gale. "I'll be back later. Come on, Spence." Without a hat he turned toward the door.

4

Idling at the end of his bar, Phil Darlington felt Cherry press against his shoulder. For the past two hours she had worn a thoughtful expression on her face and he had waited. Now she said, "I've been wondering what kind of a man this Ward Gale could be to beat Matt Roberts' time."

"Here comes Geoffry Allison," he said. "We'll ask him."

He watched Allison come in and stop at the crowded bar, amused at how the meticulous banker picked the widest, vacant place. Allison was a strange man. Running Matt Roberts' bank, he had proven himself smart and shrewd. He held himself aloof from everyone, and his habits were utterly regular.

Each night, at nine, he carefully closed the bank, walked slowly down the length of Gold, crossed and followed Washington until he reached Darlington's. Turning in he had his one drink. Then, without a word to anyone, he retraced his steps, passed the bank, and entering the Union Exchange, climbed to his room. In the year Darlington had watched him, the man had always followed the set pattern of the streets. Never once had he cut diagonally across the Square. But in spite of this, Darlington sensed an itch inside the man, some passion he struggled against. Someday that thing would break through and Darlington often wondered what course the flood would take.

Usually the gambler honored Allison's obvious desire for solitude, permitting himself only a curt nod of recognition. But tonight he broke the rule and moved down the bar to Allison's side, Cherry following.

"Evening, Allison," he said.

Allison started to frown, then his eyes moved beyond Darlington. He lifted his hat and said, "Good evening, Miss Darlington. Good evening, Phil."

Darlington signaled the bartender. "This one's on the house."

"Thank you," said Allison. He smiled, faintly. "It's been a wearing evening."

Darlington said, idly, "I can imagine, with Roberts cutting his water rates. What made him do that? This new engineer, Gale?"

"He's no engineer," said Allison. "The man's a swindler. A friend of Spencer Morehouse."

"What does a swindler look like?" asked Cherry.

"I don't know," said Allison. "I've never seen him."

"If you'll turn around," said Darlington, "you can see him. He just came in the front door."

Allison looked around. Spencer Morehouse was coming along the bar, a tall, rangy, redheaded man pacing beside him. And Allison disliked the redhead instantly when Cherry Darlington said, "There comes a man, Phil. You can pick them out a long way off. There aren't many in this world."

Her brother had no chance to answer. Morehouse had paused before him. "Hello, Darlington," he said.

Darlington said, softly, "You still in town, Spencer?"

Gale swept Morehouse gently aside. "Why wouldn't he be, Darlington?"

"I don't know," said Darlington. "It was just a remark."

"Mr. Gale," said Cherry, quickly. "You're a stranger in town. Let me show you the house."

Gale looked at her. "No," he said.

"Gale," said Darlington, reprovingly, "my sister, Cherry."

Gale gave the girl a longer look, impressed by what he saw. She met his eyes squarely, a little mockingly. "How do you do," Gale said.

Darlington, faintly amused now, said, "And Mr. Gale, have you met Geoffry Allison? Geoffry Allison is an important man in camp. He runs the Roberts Bank. Mr. Allison, Mr. Gale."

Geoffry Allison was embarrassed. Gale gave him a curt nod and showed no other interest and Darlington made a note of the effect the slight had on the man. The banker was proud, he thought, and had a tender skin.

Morehouse, bright and watchful, said, "This is not a social call."

"That's right," said Gale.

"What's the matter?" said Darlington. "Don't you like our place?" He was stiff and offended.

"I don't like the way it's run," said Gale. "You got Wilson Kellogg drunk tonight."

Darlington said, softly, "I never interfere with the habits of my customers. In this country, Mr. Gale, a man does what it pleases him to do. This is a public bar. If a man wants to drink, that is his privilege."

"Not," said Gale, "when he is my father-in-law. Don't serve him again."

"And if I do?"

Gale said, without any anger, "Running a place like this, you're too smart to ask that kind of a question." He motioned to Morehouse. "Come on, Spence."

Allison stepped a little aside to let them pass. Darlington was silent. Cherry said, a little breathlessly, "I told you he was a man. And he's dangerous, too. If he told me to do something, I'd do it."

Allison turned and stared after Gale with an unprecedented show of interest. Remembering what Cherry had just said, he was suddenly jealous. But his analytical mind considered the possibilities of such a situation and found them interesting.

Unconscious of this interest, Gale moved out onto Washington and stood with his back to the lighted windows, staring out across the dark Square with its brooding Hangman's Oak.

"How soon can we call a miners' meeting, Spence?"

"It won't do any good," said Morehouse.

"I didn't ask you that."

"Tomorrow night," said Morehouse, crossly, "if I send out riders. Did you ever see a more beautiful woman than Cherry Darlington?"

"Huh?" said Gale. "What are you talking about?"

"Some day," said Morehouse, "I'm going to have to kill Geoffry Allison. I don't like the way he looks at her."

6.

At six o'clock, Gale and Prudence left the house and moved down Adams Street toward the already crowded Square. Prudence clung proudly to Gale's arm.

"Don't worry, Ward," she said. "You've never heard my father speak. The miners believe in him."

"We'll see," said Gale, as they came into the Square and turned along Silver to the steps of Aruup's store.

The lean, stooped figure of the merchant stood in the door opening and he raised his hat. "Good evening, Prudence."

"Good evening," she said. "Have you met my husband?"

"This afternoon," said Aruup, and gave Gale his dry, friendly smile. "You better stay with me, Prudence. You can see from these steps."

"A good idea," said Gale, and moved away into the crowd.

All day, riders had ridden the rough country, combing the dry gulches, carrying the word of the meeting to the farthest camp of the mining district. To Gale the reaction was amazing. The Square was packed, giving him his first inkling of how many people lived in the surrounding hills, his first inkling of the burning interest the miners took in their affairs. This was truly democracy at work.

He pushed his way through the crowd toward the band stand beside the Hangman's Oak. Kellogg was already on the platform talking to the alcalde and the chiefs of the volunteer fire departments. At the rear of the raised floor,

Shultz's Silver Cornet Band were testing their horns and lungs. Above the sound and the swelling murmur of the crowd, Kellogg greeted him.

"Here you are, Ward." He put a hand on Gale's shoulder. "Gentlemen, my son-in-law."

Wilson Kellogg had been born to stand before crowds. A slight man, ordinarily drab, physically colorless, like an actor he came to life only before an audience. This was his proper place, standing before the miners who loved him, ready to make the speech of the evening.

He turned and signaled Marvin Shultz. The bandleader waved his horn. The music started. The audience fell silent. When the last note floated out, Kellogg raised his hand.

"Fellow citizens of the future state capital of California, I call you together once more. You honor me by your response."

He stopped as wave on wave of cheers beat against the building fronts facing the Square. Gale was amazed at the magnetic spell this slight man had upon the crowd.

"Eight months ago," said Kellogg, "I pointed out that the ruinous water rates were strangling the growth of this community and that there was only one solution, that we must build a competing ditch. A ditch owned by you miners to service you with your own water. Those plans are now formulated. A company has been organized. Already a number of shares have been sold. An engineer has come in to oversee the work. Modesty forbids me to dwell upon his virtues, since on the journey from San Francisco, he became a member of my family."

Here again he was forced to pause. These miners, living often for months in lonely isolation, seeing a woman but seldom, loved the thought of a wedding. Shouts rose from the crowd.

"Let's see the bridegroom!"

"Let's hear him talk!"

Kellogg motioned and Gale rose, unwillingly. It had been no part of his plan to talk. But he could not deny the crowd. He looked down upon the bearded faces, then over toward Aruup's store. Prudence waved and he raised his hand in return. He came back to the miners, then.

"Last night," he said, "your water rates were reduced and

there was only one reason for that reduction. Matt Roberts feared the competition of the new water company· and hoped to stop it before we ever got started. He won't." He brought a fist smashing down upon the railing of the stand. "No matter what he does, he won't stop it. Somehow, some way, I will build another water ditch."

He stepped back and they cheered him as if they recognized in his brevity a stubborn purpose. Before Kellogg could rise to take back the meeting, Geoffry Allison swung up the platform steps and turned to face the crowd.

"A moment, please!" Matt Roberts' banker never lost his studied dignity. "This is an open miners' meeting. I have a right to be heard." His voice was calm and clipped and assured.

"Go ahead!" shouted someone.

"This second water company is going to cost a fortune. Mr. Kellogg mentioned that they had already sold some stock. What he has failed to mention is that they need to sell thousands of additional shares in order to complete their ditch." He turned. "Is that right, Mr. Gale?"

"Certainly," said Gale. "Every man out there knows that."

"You see," said Allison. "It's money they're asking for. When Matt Roberts built his ditch, he used his own funds. Without that ditch, this camp never would have grown. Now that he has paid off part of his investment, Mr. Roberts has voluntarily lowered your rates. But these men, these penniless adventurers are asking you to give gold into their hands. Gold you dug out of the ground. Gold you slaved for. Gold you came six thousands miles to gain. Now they're asking you to give it to them. I don't believe you're that foolish."

Allison drew no cheers. It was the silence he caused that worried Gale. He looked appealingly at Kellogg and knew instantly they had lost. Kellogg had the feel of crowds, the sense of the mob reaction. The man made no effort to rise. It was Morehouse who stepped up.

Small, almost dainty, he stood alone at the platform's edge and the silence came up as if to push him back. But he merely smiled down, rocking slowly on his small feet, standing there so long, that everyone was forced to look at him.

"We've heard a lot of words tonight," he said, in a conversational tone. "As speeches, they should be written down and preserved. Not for their factual content, but for their beautiful rhetoric." He paused and smiled as if he shared a joke with them and they snickered back at him.

"But we didn't come here to listen to beautiful phrases. We came here to discuss facts. And so far, facts have been strangely missing. This is the richest square mile in the world. That is a fact. You made it so by your labor. That is a fact. And out of every dollar that you have produced, you have been forced to pay an exorbitant portion because Matt Roberts controls the water. That is a fact.

"But water runs free in the Stanislaus. Other people in the world have the foresight of Matt Roberts. These men are not unfamiliar with the situation in Carolina. For a long time, they have planned to get a foothold in the mining country. They control some of the biggest banks in the world. And right now, one of their representatives is in San Francisco, waiting for word from me. That is a fact.

"If you boys don't wish to put up the money, they'll finance a second water company. But frankly, Mr. Gale and I had hoped that we could keep this in local control. That by pooling your resources, you miners could own and operate your own ditch. It's for you to decide. But you'll have to act quickly. If international bankers take over, your chance will be forever gone. That is a fact."

He moved back, raising his hands as a signal he was through.

Allison stepped into the doubtful pause. "A pretty speech," he said. "But curiously lacking in the very facts Morehouse talks about. I dare him to mention the name of this mysterious, international bank that is so eager to come into Carolina."

Morehouse straightened his coat, then said blandly to Allison, "Thanks for calling the oversight to my attention. I did neglect to mention the banker's name. Perhaps some of you never heard of them. I'm speaking of the House of Rothschild."

Allison started. Over his calm, white face came a look of unaccustomed surprise. He masked it quickly. "You're joking."

"I never joke," said Morehouse, hugely pleased with himself. He turned and lifted a hand to Marvin Schultz. The band started up and closed the meeting out.

2

When the music was done, the miners turned toward the saloons across Washington Street. During the meeting the places of entertainment had been deserted and each doorway was filled with watching bartenders, dealers and girls.

The lower denizens of the Concho choked the alley entrances, staring curiously across the deadline at what was happening in the Square.

Darlington and his sister stood a little apart, listening with close attention to the distant words, weighing their effect upon the crowd. They too were involved, for their fortunes were linked closely with those of Roberts and they knew that their very existence depended upon the whims of those in power.

During Allison's speech, Darlington smiled. But after Spencer Morehouse had begun to talk, he turned, frowning; and at the mention of the House of Rothschild he said quietly, "I wonder if he's lying?"

"If he is," said Cherry, "he's running a good bluff. We could use that man, Phil."

"No," said Darlington. "He would never work for anyone except himself. But he's smart. He saved the meeting tonight. Allison had them convinced. Now they're not sure."

But Cherry wasn't listening. Gale and Morehouse had left the platform and with Derksen opening a path for them, made their way across the Square to where Prudence waited.

"I told you everything would be all right," she said. "You wanted to give up too easily."

Morehouse gave her his slow, secretive smile. Gale said, "I'll take you home. Then I have to come back down town. Spencer has opened an office next to the Holbrook House. We should be there to talk to anyone interested." He turned to Morehouse. "Get hold of Wilson and keep him with you. I'll be back in a few minutes."

Prudence said to Morehouse, "Why didn't you tell us

about outside bankers being interested? When my father went to San Francisco to talk to bankers, you ruined his chances and made me think bad of you."

"I'd do it again," said Morehouse, thinking fast. "If you heard what I said, we don't want outside bankers in here. We want this ditch to be owned by the miners. We'll only call in the banks as a last resort." He turned quickly away before she could continue her questioning.

Gale frowned over the exchange and was unusually silent during the walk home. He was troubled by Spencer's actions, but he was more troubled by his wife's attitude when he left her at the house.

She kissed him. "Please don't be late," she said. "I'm getting tired of this water ditch. It takes your time. I hardly see you. It's even hard to realize we're married."

"You want the ditch, too," he said, with unnecessary brusqueness, and saw the hurt in her eyes. "I'll get back as soon as I can."

He left the house and walked rapidly back to the Square. The new water company office was thronged with men. But looking around, Gale realized there were few miners present. Here was the alcalde, the firemen and members of the band making holiday on the whisky Morehouse had furnished. These were not investors. He signaled the small man and, together, they stepped out onto the street and moved slowly up the dark sidewalk.

"If the miners believed what you said," said Gale, "you've put us in a beautiful hole. No one will want to invest. They'll let your mysterious banker do it. House of Rothschild, indeed."

"Look," said Morehouse. "Will you be practical? Roberts and Allison already had us beaten. I pulled it out of the fire. We still have a chance. Roberts doesn't know whether I'm lying or not."

"I know you're a liar," said Gale. "Rothschild has no representatives in San Francisco."

"Maybe yes, maybe no. They have representatives all over the world. But that isn't the important thing. Our one remaining chance is to stampede the miners into buying stock. If they think other people are interested, they'll be more eager to invest."

It was logical and Gale had no answer at the moment. They walked on in silence. Morehouse finally said, "There's a thing that bothers me, Ward. A minute ago you called me a liar. That's all right. But not the way you said it. I remember you married Prudence Kellogg at Simmons' Tent. Don't call me a liar again."

Gale reached out and laid a rough hand on Spencer's shoulder. Morehouse made no effort to jerk away. For an instant they stood thus, in the half darkness; then Gale let his hand fall.

"All right, Spence," he said. "Maybe you're right. Maybe not."

3

Roberts stood at the darkened window of his room on the top floor of the Union Exchange Hotel. The whole building was his, as was most of the property on this side of the Square, and he had fitted the rooms up without regard to cost. There was nothing finer, even in San Francisco.

From this vantage point he looked out across the town, calculating its growth and turning that growth to his advantage. He was frowning now as he watched the miners flow out of the Square.

Forever alert to any threat against his position, he had to take Morehouse seriously. To do otherwise would be too much of a gamble. And Matt Roberts never took a chance if he could do a thing a safer way. Retreating to his writing table, he penned a note to his agents in San Francisco. This would go out on the morning stage.

That done, he returned to the window and stood there until the crowd had dissolved even from the saloons and the last departing miners had vanished toward the hills. Then he descended to the deserted street and made his way across Washington and into Darlington's.

Already the big overhead lamps had been turned low. A few stragglers lingered at the bar or made one last chance at the tables. The tired girls were gone and Darlington and Cherry sat at the rear, tallying the night's receipts. This was a chore Darlington enjoyed and never left to others. He had a real love of money. He liked to handle it. It annoyed him to be interrupted at this pleasant task and he did not trouble to hide his annoyance as he raised his eyes to Roberts'.

"You here?"

Matt Roberts seldom crossed Washington Street. Although much of the property flanking the twisting alleys was his he left the control of the district to Darlington. Theirs was an unwritten partnership. Roberts had no direct financial interest in the gambling hall, but he did derive large revenues from the rental of his buildings and it was to his advantage that the district be well handled.

This was an understanding then between them and at certain times Roberts had called upon Darlington for aid just as the gambler had invoked Roberts' help occasionally in dealing with the authorities. Therefore, Roberts had no hesitation in speaking openly, even with Cherry present.

Unasked, he sat down at the table and said, "Did you hear the speeches, tonight?"

"I heard them," said Darlington.

"Gale," said Roberts, "has to go."

"It was Morehouse who spoke about the bankers," Darlington said.

"Morehouse is smart," admitted Roberts. "But Gale is the dangerous one. Find a man who can catch him in the hills. Let him understand that Gale's body is not to be discovered. I want it to appear that Gale ran away. Some money will disappear from my bank at the same time. I want Gale branded as a thief."

"Ah," said Darlington. "You hate him."

"No," said Roberts. "It's merely good business that he should disappear."

"I'm not a child, Matt," said Darlington. "Don't tell me that. He married your woman."

"Damn you," Roberts said, and shoved back his chair. "Keep your nose out of my affairs."

"I see what I see," said Darlington. "It's her you want convinced. You don't care whether the miners think Gale is a thief or not."

"Do what I say," said Roberts.

"Sure," said Darlington. "I'll do what you say, as long as it serves our purpose."

Roberts looked at the man for a long time. "Be sure of that," he said.

Not until he had disappeared through the doorway, did Darlington speak. Then he glanced reflectively at his sister. "You're twenty-three," he said. "It's time you were married."

Startled, Cherry looked at him, searchingly. "What are you thinking about now?"

"I was thinking," said Phil, "that Roberts needs a woman. If you married him, this whole town would belong to us."

"Do you want the town that bad, Phil?"

"No," he said, instantly. "It was just a thought."

"Do you want to see me happy, Phil?"

"Yes. I wish there was a way to make you happy. That's the only thing I dislike about my position here. The slights you are forced to endure from the hypocrites on the other side of Washington Street."

"They're not important," she told him. "If you want to make me happy, don't do what Roberts asks. Don't kill the redhead."

Darlington studied her. "Gale's married," he said.

"I'm not so sure. There's more to marriage than the ceremony. Don't do what Roberts said."

Darlington bowed his head. "If that's the way you feel."

She reached across the table and pressed his hand. "Thanks, Phil. I don't ask for many things."

Thoughtfully, he watched her cross the room and mount the stairs to their quarters above. When she was gone, he sighed and motioned to the head bartender. "Find Charley."

The man removed his spotted apron and left the saloon. Darlington sat in the half dark, waiting, fondling the stacks of gold on the table before him. It was a full hour before the bearded man drifted in through the side door. He glanced around, uncertain, then sidled over to the table.

"All right, Charley," Darlington pushed out a chair. "Sit down."

The man slid into the seat, never taking his beady eyes from Darlington's face. "You wanted to see me?"

Wordlessly, Darlington counted out five of the twenty dollar square golden slugs. He weighed them in his hand as if hating to part with them, then spread them out before

Royer. "The man," he said, "is the new engineer, Gale. Get him in the hills. I don't want his body found."

He watched Royer pick up the slugs, watched the man bob his head and then turn to leave, and there was a faint smile on Darlington's lips. Gale he thought, would cause Roberts no more trouble, but of far more importance, he would no longer color Cherry's thoughts.

4

Ward Gale lay awake through the long hours of the night, unmoving beside his wife. In her sleep Prudence had thrown an arm across his body, her palm caressingly against his cheek. He did not move because he did not wish to awaken her, and his muscles grew stiff and rigid with his unaccustomed stillness.

In the shaft of moonlight he could see that she smiled in her sleep, and he had a sudden unexpected sense of tenderness toward her.

He thought how different his feelings might have been had they met under normal circumstances. But he realized now that all his thinking was colored by one thing, his hatred of Matt Roberts, and that in his every contact with her, that hatred intruded to spoil the fullness of his reactions.

But he had managed to play his part well. When they had returned to the house that evening she had talked happily of their future plans. The trouble was that he visualized no future for himself. He would break Roberts, and then he would kill him. The thought had been growing on him again for the full day. After the killing anything that happened to him would be anti-climactic. And without hope of the future, he had nothing.

He had to hold himself apart from Prudence. He had to keep her as it were at arm's length lest any feeling for her might weaken his final resolve.

He wondered, lying there, if she would remarry when he was gone. She probably would. Most women did, especially on the frontier where there were never enough women to go around. And the thought that she might, that she might sleep in this very bed brought to him a strange feeling of jealousy which he found it hard to brush away.

Finally when grey morning light outlined the window he could remain quiet no longer and tried to slip from the bed.

But the girl roused and lay watching him as he hurriedly dressed, her eyes still warm with sleep. "So early," she said.

"I've got to make a start," he told her. "The ditch must begin at the Stanislaus, not here. I don't know the country. I must survey it before I can make any decisions."

"Morehouse knows the country."

Gale shook his head. "Spencer is needed in town. Besides I can't see through another man's eyes." He moved toward the door, but she stopped him.

"You forgot to kiss me."

He turned back to the bed almost reluctantly and taking her shoulders between his big hands bent over until his lips were against hers.

She sensed his reluctance as he straightened. "What's happened, Ward? Are you displeased with something that I've done?"

He managed his smile. "Of course not. It's just that there is so much work to do."

She looked at him carefully, still not satisfied. "Ward, let's not ever have so much to do that we haven't time for each other."

"Of course not," he lied, and turning left the room. He paused for his hat in the lower floor, then stepped out to the street and walked rapidly to the hotel. He climbed to the second floor and routed out Morehouse.

"What the devil you doing up this time of the morning?" the little man complained. "Don't you ever stay in bed?"

"There's something to do," said Gale. "I want a horse. I want you to draw me a map of the country; you must have some idea where this ditch should go."

"Kellogg had a survey run," said Morehouse. "Get the map from him."

"You get it," said Gale. "I'll meet you at the livery in half an hour."

Morehouse sat back down on the edge of the bed and stared up at him. "What are you up to? Did you have a fight with Prudence?"

"Of course not." Gale was impatient.

"Something's wrong," said Morehouse. "You're running away. There's no need of you going out into the hills. We can send Derksen. Your place is here, helping me raise money."

Gale shook his head. "You and Kellogg can do that better than I can. I have to get away, Spence. I want a chance to think."

"It's a little late to start thinking, isn't it?" said Morehouse. "You should have done your thinking at Simmons' Tent, before you married her."

"You look out for yourself," said Gale. "I'll look out for me. And by the way. If you collect any money while I'm gone, you be sure that it's here when I get back."

Spencer's smile was barbed. "You look out for yourself," he said. "I'll look out for me. If you're worried about me and any money I might collect, maybe you'd better stay here in town, with your lovely wife, and watch me."

Gale hit him with his open hand. Spencer's head rocked to one side, but he made no move to defend himself. He sat for a long time, staring up at the bigger man. Slowly he rubbed his reddened cheek and said, "I'm sorry, Ward." It was impossible to judge what he meant. "I'll get the map. There's some notes I have, too." Crossing to a chest of drawers he took out a leather bound field book and handed it to Ward.

"Spence . . ." Gale said, staring at the book.

"Forget it," said Morehouse. "Don't give it another thought."

"I realize," said Gale, doggedly, "that I'm leaving you the bad end of the job. After the speech you made last night, everybody will be watching you. If your banker fails to show up. . . ."

"Don't worry," said Morehouse. "I'll make out. I'll make out. I'll do my thinking first so I won't have any regrets later."

5

Gale camped that night at Dead Man's Bar with four miners who were ground sluicing. Their shack was tight and well built and they were congenial. After the pan biscuits and bear steak had been put away, Gale sat back with a scalding cup of strong coffee and questioned them.

They knew the country well. They knew the basin twenty miles up the North Fork which would serve for the dam site. None, of course, knew the grades and contours accurately enough to be certain that water could be brought down by a gravity flow ditch. But one of the miners had been a lawyer and he outlined the position, graphically.

"It's more than an engineering problem," he told Gale. "Roberts, by right of possession, owns the right-of-way on which his flume is carried. In order for you to come into Carolina with a gravity flow ditch, it will be necessary for you to cross the Roberts' right-of-way."

"We'll cross it," said Gale.

"You'll have to use one of two methods," said the lawyer. "One is by force. The second by law. By law it will be a long, drawn out process."

"We'll cross," Gale said, "one way or another," and they liked the way he said it.

Gale could be a ready talker when he chose and he talked now. It was a relief to talk to men, to put the thoughts of Prudence out of his mind.

He was up before daylight, picking his way along the canyon rim, followed the line of Roberts' flume, studying the workmanship and marveling at the difficulties that had been overcome. This was no simple operation. It was a problem to tax the ingenuity of any man.

By the third night he had a good general idea of the country. Constantly he was surprised by the number of people he met in the timbered hills. Each sand bar had its quota of gold miners lifting water from the river with their Chinese water wheels, using it to sluice out their gravel.

They were men from all walks of life, from all experiences. Laborers. Doctors. Even ministers.

Roberts' dam was a log structure, earth-filled and very tight. The intake ditch came off three hundred feet above the dam and by drilling, Roberts had lowered a natural break in the rock wall. Thence the ditch followed the canyon side at a much less pitch than the river so that it came level with the rim, east of Carolina. From there it was flumed across a steep gulch on a timbered trestle, went through a sharp cut in the limestone shoulder and came out on the hillside a good four hundred feet above town, running down in an open earth ditch to another trestle at Yankee Hill.

But the problem for the second ditch was not so simple. Gale found the basin which the miners had described and knew it well suited to his purpose. Then using the notes of Kellogg's survey, he back tracked, criss-crossing the rough country, hunting for a workable grade.

His horse went a little lame and he worked two days on foot, but he found what he wanted. The pitch of the North Fork canyon was sharper than that of the middle stream and not so deep. He could lift his flume over the canyon wall within ten miles of the dam site, carry it along a hogback, bridge three gulches and run down a natural wash to the Middle Fork canyon where he would be five hundred feet above the tumbling stream.

He would turn and follow the canyon wall to the point the Roberts' ditch branched off for Carolina. It would be necessary then to build a bridge to cross Roberts' flume and come in to the north of it, recrossing the flume below Yankee Hill.

There was one difficulty. Roberts had come down the south wall of the canyon which sloped sufficiently to carry his ditch. But on the side Gale would be forced to use, the rock face, in places, fell abruptly for a thousand feet. There was only one solution, to hang the flume from this rock face, using iron supports.

On his last night out, the first he had camped alone, Gale sat staring into his tiny fire. The magnitude of the problem had captured his interest and he came to with a start to realize that for at least twenty-four hours he had given no thought to his hatred of Matt Roberts. There would be a satisfaction in building this ditch for the mere sake of building.

He was up at daybreak, turning his horse toward town. The rising hills boxed him in and the scent of the pines was sweet. He began to understand his wife's love for this country. It grew on a man. It would be nice to ride these hills with her, to sit with her by a fire at night, but those were impossible thoughts. There was nothing beyond his settlement with Matt Roberts. These last ten days had brought no answer to the real problem he had set out to think about.

At noon, he reached the Middle Fork, let his horse drink, stripped off his clothes and plunged into the rushing water. It battered at his body, sending him against the stones and he fought it, enjoying the stimulating freedom. Then, refreshed, he dressed and took the curving trail upward toward the distant rim.

When he topped out of the canyon he dismounted to let the horse rest and as he did so he jumped as a boy slipped silently out of the bushes.

"Hiya!" said the youngster. He had a full game sack on his shoulder and a long rifle in the crook of his arm.

"Hello," said Gale. "Where you from?"

"Carolina town. I'm hunting. I hunt for French's Restaurant."

Gale said, idly, "What's the news in town?"

The boy dropped his sack and hunkered down on his heels. "Nothin' much." Then he brightened. "They're having fights tonight. Yankee Sullivan and the Philadelphia Kid, with a bear and bull bait, first. Sullivan will beat him."

"That all?"

"Well, there's a new bank."

"What new bank?"

The boy ran his hand through his tousled hair. "Them Rothschild fellows, from over Europe way. Paw says Matt Roberts don't like 'em none too well."

Gale started with surprise. "The Rothschilds? How far is it to town?"

"About four miles," said the boy. "Some call it five."

Gale rose and swung up into the saddle. "Be seeing you. Luck."

"So long, Mister," said the boy. "See you at the fights, huh?"

"Sure," said Gale, and urged his tired horse forward, wondering what Morehouse had done now.

The trail was rough and the horse had a tendency to falter, but Gale pushed it on, driven by impatience. A little while later he came out into a bare space a good two hundred yards across, a natural cup surrounded by high, timbered ridges.

Crossing this, the animal began to limp again and Gale was forced to dismount. As he swung down, a rifle cracked from the ridge to the right, and a bullet whined across the saddle he had just emptied. Startled, the horse reared, almost jerking Gale from his feet. He fought the reins desperately, trying to drag the animal down. His own rifle was in the saddle boot.

The gun from the ridge spoke again. The heavy slug made a wet sound as it struck the plunging horse. The animal screamed, pawed two staggering steps and fell beside a low brush clump.

Gale dived behind the fallen horse. He dragged the rifle from the saddle boot and laid the barrel across the animal's carcass. Laying his cheek against the stock, he studied a drifting wisp of smoke on the ridge and waited.

Nothing happened. When he felt the strain too long, he inched up for a better look. The rifle cracked again, this time behind him. The bullet bored through the brush at his ear. Gale dropped flat and edged around the horse. The fourth shot came within inches of his boot toe, and from a different direction.

Trapped in the open, with that unseen rifleman free to move about, Gale knew he had no chance, and, realizing it, he lost all physical fear. What came to him now were three deep regrets. He should have killed Roberts on the river boat. Failing to do that he should have been more careful. And, he should have never married Prudence Kellogg. That had been the greatest mistake. There had been no need to hurt the girl. She was the last person in the world he would see hurt, and he suddenly knew that it was much more important to keep her from being hurt than it was to get Roberts. And he had to admit there was only one reason why he felt this. There was only one emotion stronger than hate. That was love.

The irony of making this discovery now was doubly bitter. She was his wife. He had held her in his arms, but never once during their relationship had he ever told her he loved her. Now that chance was gone. A bullet sliced the shirt across his shoulder.

He squirmed further around the dead animal and saw the field book sticking from the burst saddlebag. Cautiously, he worked it free. There was little time to write and little space. He wrote on the fly leaf.

"Prudence:

I love you. No matter what you hear or what men say, I love you. Spencer Morehouse thinks I married you to hurt Matt Roberts. He might even tell you that now to ease your grief. But even though it might cause you more grief, Spencer is wrong. Take comfort in the knowledge that my last thoughts were all of you. I did lie about Matt Roberts at the Tent. He has no wife. But I had to change your mind. Whatever happens, I could not have you married to that man.

Your husband,

Ward."

7.

FOR THE FIRST TIME in his life, Spencer Morehouse was troubled. Day after day he sat alone in the office of the new water company, waiting for the investors who had failed, so far, to appear. Only a few thousand dollars worth of stock had been sold and the miners, while they showed a lively interest in the water company's doings, were holding back, enjoying Matt Roberts' enforced generosity and beginning to express their doubts about foreign bankers being interested in Carolina.

Morehouse guessed shrewdly that these doubts had been planted in the men's minds by Roberts' agents. Having always earned his fortune by his wits, he knew, only too well, what he would have done in Roberts' place.

Also he understood the miners thoroughly. They were hanging back, waiting for someone to make the first move. If he could only produce a foreign banker, then he could see himself swamped with men seeking to invest, afraid that the opportunity would pass them by. But how to produce a banker, when he knew none, was quite a problem.

Both Kellogg and his daughter had already questioned him and he had succeeded in evading a direct answer. Now time was running out. He glanced at his watch and saw that the afternoon stage was due and, as he had done each day since Gale had ridden into the hills, he rose and walked outside.

A slim cheroot clamped in his thin lips, he stood with his

95

back to the sun, staring diagonally across the Square toward the Express Office. He was unconscious of the fact that Darlington stood behind him in the alley's mouth, watching as he always did, the stage's arrival.

Cherry joined her brother Phil and fastened her attention on Morehouse's small, immaculate figure. "What's he up to, Phil?"

"Who?" Darlington's thoughts had been with Charley, in the hills. Gale had been gone four days now.

"Spencer Morehouse. For the last four days he's watched the stage come in. It isn't like you to fail to notice things. What's wrong with you, Phil?"

"I saw him the first day," said Darlington. "He's pretending to watch for his banker."

"What if his banker does come in?"

"It wouldn't do any good. There won't be a second ditch."

"I'm not so sure," Cherry told him. "That redhead's been out surveying."

"That's what Morehouse says." Darlington spoke without looking at her. "But how do we know he's surveying? I think maybe he's run out. I don't think he'll ever come back."

Cherry looked at him, sharply. She started to say something then changed her mind and said, instead, "He'll be back, unless something happened to him and nothing had better happen to him, Phil. Remember that." She did not wait for the stage's arrival, but went back into the saloon, leaving her brother alone with his discomforting thoughts.

Far out on the road that came into Adams Street, a sudden flash of reflected sun told Morehouse the stage was coming in. Always before he had remained standing on the wooden walk before the water company office. But today he started diagonally across the Square, hardly conscious that he moved until he had passed the bandstand.

The stage turned the corner with a flourish, the driver sawing back on his long lines to bring the six panting horses to a plunging stop before the Express Office. Morehouse elbowed his way in, centering his attention on one of the passengers, and excitement rode up in him.

He was a man who had always played his hunches and he had the feeling of being right, now. Four of the passengers were obviously miners. The fifth might have been anything. He was carefully dressed. He looked like money, and he had the self assured air of a man who has seen many places and many things, none of them forgotten.

Morehouse waited a moment longer. If someone met the traveler, if someone knew him, this would not work. Excited, he watched the man climb down. He watched the driver throw the luggage out of the boot. The newcomer picked up his own and started alone toward the Union Exchange. Then Morehouse went after him, shoving the crowd aside and halting the man.

"Here I am," Morehouse said, loudly, "How are you? I'd begun to think you'd never get here."

The stranger stopped, a faint, inquiring smile lifted one corner of his lips. He said, "Yes?" and waited and Morehouse was pleased that the young man was reckless enough to let him go on with his obvious mistake until the time came for him to use it as an advantage or to laugh about it.

"This way," said Morehouse, and took the bags from the other's hands. "You're headed for the wrong hotel. That's Matt Roberts' house." Saying no more he turned directly across the Square, making the stranger follow him and moving so fast they were out of the crowd before the traveler could protest.

Not until they reached the water company office and Morehouse had set down the luggage, did the newcomer have a chance to ask, "What's this all about, if you don't mind!"

"I don't mind at all," said Morehouse. "Do you know anyone around here?"

"Not a soul," said the man. "And least of all you, my friend."

"You will," said Morehouse. "My name is Spencer Morehouse and I'm looking for a man to help me play a joke on this town."

The stranger laughed. "Richard P. Telfair at your service." He bowed a little. "Traveling in boots and ladies shoes for Hamm's of Cincinnati. One of the oldest houses in the business." He looked at Spencer's polished boots and smiled.

"But I see you know my line. Now suppose you tell me yours."

Morehouse handed him a cigar and eased him into the desk chair. "All I ask, Telfair, is ten minutes of your time. I'm going to tell you an amusing story." He went right ahead, telling Telfair about the water company, without mentioning the original swindle and leaving out Gale's trouble with Roberts.

"So you see," he added, "I promised these miners a banker. There isn't any banker, of course. All I want to do is to stir them into investing in their own company. If they think you represent the House of Rothschild, they'll come rushing in to buy stock. I'll pay you well for posing as a banker for a few days. But I'll never be able to pay you as much as the satisfaction you'll get from the knowledge that you, and you alone, helped these poor struggling men to help themselves." He took a handkerchief from his pocket and dabbed gently at his eyes.

Telfair grinned. "You move me deeply, Mr. Morehouse, and I haven't had any fun since I hit this country. But one thing. If I go into this I expect to be treated with the courtesy and dignity becoming the representative of a great banking establishment."

"Anything you want," said Morehouse, agreeably. "I'll arrange for a room for you at the Holbrook House and pay all expenses. You do your own talking, but just remember two things. You don't like Matt Roberts and his methods or his bank. And you are interested in a second water ditch."

2

Prudence Gale walked into the water company office, followed by Ben Derksen. Seeing a stranger seated at the desk, she stopped. "I'm sorry," she said to Spencer Morehouse. "I didn't know you were busy."

"Come in. Come in, my dear," said Morehouse. "This is the big day. May I introduce Mr. Richard P. Telfair, the Carolina representative of the House of Rothschild. Mr. Telfair, Prudence Gale."

Telfair rose, bowing. "This," he said, "is an unexpected pleasure."

"It's a pleasure for me," said Prudence, warmly. "I'll have to tell my father you're here, Mr. Telfair. You must come to supper tonight. You bring him, Spencer."

"Sure," said Morehouse. He beamed at Telfair with all the creative pride of an artist looking at a portrait he had long imagined. But Telfair was paying no attention to him.

"We'll be there, Madam," said Telfair. "We'll be there."

"Thank you," said Prudence. "And now if you'll excuse me, I'll go and find my father."

When she was gone, Telfair drew a long breath. "Spencer, my boy, you couldn't drive me out of town with wild horses. I'm here to stay. I've been looking for a girl like her, all my life. Who is she?"

Ben Derksen shifted his feet. "Why I guess you better be careful about saying that around, Mr. Telfair," he said. "I guess Mr. Gale wouldn't like you to talk that way about his wife."

"His wife?" said Telfair. "Don't say that. You mean she's married?"

"Why you bet she's married," said Ben. "And the man she married licked Chauncey Burns. He's a big tough redhead and I'd hate to have him mad at me."

Telfair, disappointed, looked from Derksen to Morehouse. "On second thought," he said, "maybe I won't stay. Maybe you better find another man, Mr. Morehouse."

"Look," said Morehouse, quickly. "Don't take Ben seriously. Sure she's married, but it doesn't mean anything. Gale's not in love with her. He only married her because Matt Roberts wanted her. You think if Gale liked her he'd be spending his honeymoon alone in the hills? And she'll find it out one of these days. When she does, you ought to be here."

"Why Spence," said Ben Derksen, shocked, "you're a liar." With one hand he caught Morehouse by the back of his coat collar and lifted him to tiptoe. "I guess I ought to break your neck. Mr. Gale wouldn't do a thing like that." He shook Morehouse until the small man's teeth rattled. "Take it back, Spence. Take it back now."

Morehouse was scared. He had always been afraid of

Derksen's strength at close quarters. "All right, Ben," he said. "I'll take it back. I'm sorry I mentioned it."

Derksen gave him one final shake and let him go. "Why I guess you should be. I guess a man shouldn't go around talking that way."

Morehouse stepped quickly back and put his hand in his coat pocket. Rage and fear darkened his face. "Ben," he said, quietly, "don't ever lay your hands on me again. And now I'm going to take back what I just took back to get away from you. I'm right about Gale, you understand. Now forget it and get the hell out of here."

Derksen moved his head slowly from side to side. His big hands worked. "Why I don't know what's the matter with you, Spencer," he said. "But you're still lying. I'll catch you without that gun some day and make you take it back again." He turned then and shambled out of the office, a fat man in baggy clothes, suddenly tired and disillusioned.

Slowly he moved down Silver, not conscious of the people he brushed out of his way, and turning onto Adams, followed it to Kellogg's house. On the porch he knew a moment's hesitation, then he knocked and waited unhappily until Prudence opened the door for him.

"Why Ben," she said, startled by his face. "What's happened?"

Ben removed his round shapeless hat and twisted it slowly in his big hands. "Miss Prudence, how much does Spencer Morehouse mean to your water company? Could you build it without him?"

Quick alarm came up into the girl's eyes. "Ben! What's happened to Spencer?"

"Why nothing, yet," said Ben. "But can you get along without him?"

"Yes," she said, uncertainly, "I guess we could."

Derksen showed relief. "Why that's fine," he said. "Then I can go ahead and kill him."

"Ben!" cried Prudence. "Have you lost your mind? What's he done?"

"Why he's just been talking around," Derksen said.

"Talking around? What did he say?"

"Well, I don't like to tell you."

"You'll tell me," she said. "What is he saying?"

"Well, he told a man that Mr. Gale don't love you. He said Mr. Gale just married you to get even with Matt Roberts. He said . . ." the words died in Derksen's throat. The girl had started to laugh. "He said . . ." Derksen went on, doggedly, "that that's the reason Mr. Gale's gone out in the hills."

Prudence stopped laughing. She put out a hand and laid it on Ben's arm. And in the long time they stood there, Ben felt her weight lean more and more against him until he knew she had no strength of her own, remaining. Hurt grew in her eyes until he wanted to turn and run from the sight of it. He had made a mistake. Morehouse had been right.

"Why it looks to me," he said, the words dragging out of him, "like I was fixing to kill the wrong man."

Prudence pulled back from him. "Well don't ever kill Spencer Morehouse for what he said," she flared.

"Why I guess not," said Ben. "I guess I'll kill Gale."

The hurt look faded from her eyes. And what came to take its place, Ben had never seen before. It was anger without heat and more terrible because of it. Her eyes became bright and shiny, without depth or room for deep feeling.

"No, Ben," she said. "I want you to help Mr. Gale. I want this water ditch built, no matter what happens. That's for my father. As for Mr. Gale, I'll take care of him myself. And please, Ben, don't ever mention this to anyone, not even Mr. Gale. Promise me?"

"Why I promise," said Ben, and had difficulty in speaking. "But if the time ever comes, Miss Prudence. . . ."

"Yes, Ben. If the time ever comes, I'll tell you."

She watched him trudge away and when he had finally disappeared, she followed him along Adams, continuing on past the Square to enter Matt Roberts' bank.

Allison was at the high counting table, Roberts at the desk in the corner. He turned, and seeing Prudence, showed surprise.

"Come in, Prudence," he said. "Come in."

"Can I see you alone?" she asked.

"Take half an hour," said Roberts, without looking at Allison.

Geoffry Allison rose, removed his sateen wristlets deliberately, then slowly put on his broadcloth coat. He was a man who never appeared on the street in his shirt sleeves. Without a glance toward the girl, he picked up his beaver hat and stepped out into the last rays of the afternoon sun.

"Well?" said Roberts.

"I want some truths, Matt," Prudence said. "You knew Ward Gale before you came here, didn't you?"

He searched her face carefully, making his decision. "We knew each other. Yes. I suppose I should have told you before, but hated to admit the mistake of having known such a man."

She sighed a little, knowing that once started on the truth he would probably keep on. It made it harder for her to ask her next question. "Are you married, Matt? Do you have a wife and two children in Boston?"

"Me?" said Roberts. His laugh was so instantaneous, she knew what the right answer was before he even said, "Where in the world did you get that idea? Oh . . ." his face hardened. "Ward Gale told you."

"Yes," she said. "Ward Gale told me."

"He lied," said Roberts.

"I know he did," said Prudence. "Can you tell me any more about him?"

"Plenty," said Roberts, thinking of Charley's mission in the hills. "It's too bad you waited until he ran out on you."

Prudence stiffened a little. "What makes you think he ran away?"

"I know it," said Roberts. "I know he'll never come back. It's too bad you never asked me about him before this, Prudence."

3

The next morning, Spencer Morehouse lay abed late, thinking about the preceding evening. Never since first meeting her, had he known Prudence to be as entertaining, as vivacious as she had been last night at supper. Spurred by her charm, Richard Telfair had thoroughly convinced Wilson Kellogg that he was Rothschild's representative. The man had talked glowingly of eastern cities and European capitals and Morehouse chuckled at the memory. Telfair was a convincing liar and it was obvious he would do anything to build himself up in the eyes of Wilson Kellogg's daughter.

Spencer rose finally, taking his usual care with his toilet, and then walked down the hall to Telfair's room. It was empty. Concerned, Morehouse went on down stairs and out to the street.

The first thing that caught his eye was a huge sign, the paint still wet, over the doorway of the water company office.

"Rothschild and Company—Bankers and Dealers In International Exchange. Correspondents in New York, Philadelphia And Abroad. Richard P. Telfair, Local Manager And Partner."

For an instant, Morehouse refused to believe his eyes. Then anger flared up in him. This shoe salesman certainly had his nerve. This could easily wreck all their hopes of selling stock. Morehouse felt in his pocket, then he moved quickly to the office entrance and pushed in.

Telfair sat at a desk in the corner. Behind him, against the wall, stood an empty packing case. He looked up and smiled, engagingly.

"Ah! Good morning, Spencer. Are you the first depositor?"

Morehouse did not speak until he had reached the desk. Staring down at Telfair, he said, "Aren't you reaching out a little far to impress that girl? Who told you that you were a banker? What do you think will happen when the people learn you're nothing but a shoe salesman? I don't like people who do things without consulting me."

"That's too bad," said Telfair, unconcerned.

"For you it is," said Morehouse. "All I have to do is to step onto the street and tell the first man who comes along that this is a hoax."

Telfair chuckled. "But you can't do that, Spencer. You've already told everyone I represent the Rothschilds. You'd have some difficulty in explaining your part in this business. Why not relax and play along with me? Nothing's changed. Think of the possibilities."

Spencer's quick mind was already weighing those possibilities. And the more he thought of them the more he was inclined to agree with Telfair. He wondered why it had not occurred to him before to start a bank. A bank was even better than a water company. The miners would bring in their deposits. When the deposits became big enough, he and Telfair would merely disappear. And Telfair would be blamed. Yes, the bank was a good idea. And the name Rothschild was a stroke of genius. Even in this far country, the name would build men's confidence. He began to remove his coat.

"What are we going to do for a safe?"

Telfair indicated the empty packing case. "That will do for now. We'll get someone to guard it, of course. What about Derksen? Is he honest?"

"As the day is long," said Morehouse.

Telfair said, musingly, "And I noticed yesterday that he didn't like you too well. Yes, I think Ben Derksen will be a very good guard."

Morehouse chuckled. "Don't try and insult me, Richard. Once you put Derksen to guarding the money, he won't let you have it either. It may be a little inconvenient to reason with Ben when the time comes for us to run out."

"Run out?" Telfair looked surprised, then he smiled a bit sadly. "Spencer, you have me all wrong. I'm not running out. All my life I've wanted to settle down and be somebody. Now I have the chance. I'm head of a bank. You'll never get me out of here."

Morehouse narrowed his black eyes. Carefully, he said, "Sure, I was just sounding you out, Telfair. I thought for a minute you had cooked up some swindle. I wouldn't stand for that."

"It's a funny thing," said Telfair. "I was thinking the same thing about you. I wouldn't stand for that either. It's good we understand each other."

"It's always a good thing to know what's on the other fellow's mind," murmured Morehouse and walked outside to stare up at the green hills. He wondered where Gale was. He wondered how soon Gale would be back. He wondered what Gale would say when he found out about the bank. Things were getting out of control.

4

Gale was thirsty. His shoulder bled a little where a bullet had burned his flesh. The sun was still three hours high and there was no hope in him that darkness would come in time.

The last shot had been fired from the north ridge and now Gale lay on that side of the animal, having faked a movement to circle around. He hugged the ground tight and waited, every muscle tense against the shock of a bullet.

Minutes passed. There was no sound. Finally he heard it. A twig snapped on his exposed side. He rolled, coming up on one knee, his rifle swinging. The boy hunter stood not ten yards from him.

"Hey!" the boy yelled, surprised. "Was it you Charley Royer was shooting at? I saw him and when I yelled, he run down and got on his horse."

Gale glanced around at the circling ridge. He drew a long breath and got slowly to his feet, half expecting another shot. None came. It was peaceful. Birds called again from the tree tops. Beads of perspiration popped out on his forehead and he drew a sleeve across his face, relieved.

"Thanks," he said to the boy. "Thanks for coming down. Charley Royer, did you say?"

"Why sure," said the boy. "I saw him plain as day. He's no good, Charley ain't. He's a Concho man."

"Did he see you?" said Gale.

"No sir," said the boy. "I never let Charley see me. I must have scared him when I yelled, him not knowing who I was."

"That's good," said Gale. "And don't worry about him. If he did see you, he won't ever bother you. What's the shortest way to town?"

"I'll show you, Mister. I know a short cut."

Gale stripped the saddle from the dead animal and tossed it under the clump of brush. He made a bundle of the maps and notes and field book and stuffed them into his coat. Then catching up his rifle he swung out after the boy. The sun was just going down when they came over the brow of Yankee Hill and dropped down the side gulches into Carolina.

It was dark when Gale parted company with the boy at Adams and Silver and moved on down toward Kellogg's house. A lamp burned in the parlor window, throwing its yellow radiance in a path across the porch. He wanted to call out to Prudence, but he held it back. He wanted his hands on her, he wanted her eager kisses when he told her what he had found out on this trip. Even Charley Royer could wait until after that.

Quietly, he pushed open the front door. Sounds reached him from the rear. He edged down the hall, pausing in the kitchen entrance. Prudence was at the stove, her back to him. He took two quick steps and grasped her shoulders. She stiffened.

"It's me," Gale said.

"Oh," she said, and relaxed against him. "Matt! You startled me."

For an instant, Gale stood still, unconscious that his fingers bit into the soft flesh of her shoulders. Then he let his hands fall and she turned to face him.

"Ward!" she said. "So it's you. I didn't think you'd have the nerve to come back." Her voice was level, unflurried. As if uninterested, she turned back to the stove.

Gale caught her arm and turned her back. "Wait a minute. You said Matt. Did you mean Roberts?"

"Why yes. He's coming to supper. Do you have any objections?"

"You know how I feel about Roberts."

"I know how you lied about him."

"What do you mean?"

"You lied when you told me Roberts was married."

"Who said I lied?"

"Didn't you?"

"All right, I lied. But I had a reason to lie."

"I'm sure you did," said Prudence, her voice dangerously sweet. "I'm sure you have a reason for everything you say and do. You married me to hurt Matt Roberts. It never occurred to you that it might hurt me. You didn't even care, did you? You...."

"I cared," he said. "I cared then and I care now." He gripped her shoulders again, looking at her hungrily. "Can't you tell, Prudence?"

"I can tell," she said, "that your pride's hurt because I'm entertaining Matt Roberts. Just let me tell you something, Mr. Gale. I'm going to entertain Mr. Roberts or anyone else I choose."

Gale said, bitterly, "Then I'd best get out."

"No," she told him. "This is a small town. You're my husband. Do you think I'm going to endure the scandal of you walking off and leaving me? Not for a minute. This is what you're going to do. I'll entertain whom I please and you'll like it. You'll live here on these premises. You'll see me morning and night until you get sick and tired of looking at me, but you'll never touch me. Do you understand that?"

"If I didn't love you," said Gale, "that would be an easy thing for me to do. But I do love you, so I can't stay, Prudence. I'm sorry."

She gave him a bright, hard smile. "You'll stay. If I told the miners what you've done to me, they'd hang you to the oak in the Square. You'll stay, Ward. You'll stay until I tell you to get out."

A knock at the front door cut her off. She brushed past Gale and went down the hall. He heard her greet Roberts. Then he turned blindly, and crossing the kitchen, stepped out into the night.

He stood there a moment in the dark. Never had he wanted to kill Matt Roberts more than he wanted to now. But Prudence had tied his hands. No matter what his original motive had been, if he killed Roberts now, it would seem to Carolina that he had only struck at the man because of his own wife's unfaithfulness. The only thing he could do now was to push Roberts until the man broke and came for him first.

8.

GALE WAS CERTAIN Roberts had sent Charley Royer into the hills. Moving quickly along Silver, determined to find the man, he saw the lights in the water company's office reflecting on the new sign and broke his stride to read it. Muttering he swerved and turned in, not believing what he had read.

Spencer Morehouse was at the big desk, talking to a stranger. Ben Derksen sat on the end of a packing case, fat and unmobile, a shot gun with sawed barrels resting across his thick knees.

Morehouse said, "Ward! What the devil's happened?"

"You know a man named Charley Royer?" asked Gale.

"No," said Morehouse. "Who's he?"

"I know Charley," said Derksen. "What about him?"

"He pinned me down in a clearing," said Gale. "He killed my horse and took a dozen shots at me. Where does he hang out, Ben?"

Derksen took time to answer. "Darlington's, maybe. He's close with the head bartender."

"Good enough," said Gale, and looked at the stranger.

Morehouse saw the look and smiled a little to himself. "This is Richard Telfair, Ward. Mr. Telfair, Mr. Gale. Mr. Telfair is with the Rothschilds. He's opening a bank here."

"Has it helped you sell any stock?" said Gale.

"Why no," said Morehouse. "The bank opening has given

108

the miners the idea that the Rothschilds will build the ditch."

"I told you so," said Gale, "after your speech. You're a fool, Spence. Which one of you two thought this one up?"

Morehouse bridled. "I don't know what you're talking about."

"Yes you do," Gale said. "I don't know where you found this man, but I'll bet anything you want to name, that he has no more to do with the Rothschilds than I do. What's the idea? You figuring on collecting deposits and then running out with them?"

Telfair reddened. "Now just a minute, Mr. Gale. It doesn't matter who I was. I know something about handling credit. I've always wanted to do something like this and I intend to run this bank honestly. Why else do you think I hired Derksen to guard the money?"

"Money," said Gale. "How much have you taken in?"

"Almost a hundred thousand," said Telfair. "You'd be surprised how few men trust Mr. Roberts. They've been transferring their deposits for the last five days."

Gale could not believe it. He walked over and peered into the packing case. It was half filled with stacked leather and canvas pouches. "A hundred thousand dollars!"

"A nice round sum," said Morehouse, almost smacking his lips.

Gale turned on him sharply. "But what good is it?"

"At least," said Morehouse, "we have taken it away from Roberts. He's not pleased about it. The name Rothschild has worked a regular charm in this camp."

Gale had recovered from his first surprise. "So you're in the banking business," he said, thoughtfully. "You have a hundred thousand dollars. I'm in the water business. I need a hundred thousand dollars. You loan it to me and we'll all be a going concern. I'll give you stock in the water company as collateral."

"Now wait a minute, Ward," protested Morehouse. "Let's think this over. Let's not do anything we might regret."

"I'm not talking to you," said Gale. "You're not in the banking business. The House of Rothschild wouldn't let you in one of their banks unless they tied your hands. I'm speaking to Telfair. What do you say, Mr. Banker?"

"I say no," said Telfair, instantly. "From what you've told us, you're not a good risk, Mr. Gale. And the way Morehouse tells it, stock in the water company is no better than you. Collateral, shot full of holes, has very little value. This bank will lend you no money."

Gale's mouth tightened. "You know, Telfair, what would happen if I exposed you?"

"Yes I do," said Telfair. "They'd run the bank and close me out in a few hours."

"That's right," said Gale.

"But that would ruin you, too," Telfair pointed out. "Morehouse set me up in this town as a member of the House of Rothschild. Everyone knows you're associated with Mr. Morehouse."

Morehouse laughed. "Ward," he said, "you get the funniest look on your face when you get stuck." He turned his amusement on Telfair. "But you better watch him, Dick. He got the same look on his face when I thought I had him in a corner in Stockton. He turned the tables on me. He's liable to do the same on you."

"There's nothing he can do," said Telfair, sure of himself, "without ruining his own game."

"Why don't be so sure about that," said Ben Derksen, shifting the shot gun on his knees.

Gale looked at the fat man. "Ben," he said, "I'm going to find Charley Royer. You want to come with me and watch my back?"

Derksen returned his stare. "Has finding Charley got anything to do with building a water ditch?"

Gale shook his head. "No, Ben. It's personal. Does that make any difference?"

Derksen spat into the corner. "I work here at night," he said. "I guess I could get off if it had something to do with the water ditch. But I guess I can't get off if it's personal. That's what I promised Mrs. Gale. She made me promise I'd help you build the water ditch. I'll do anything she says."

"Thanks, Ben," said Gale, Derksen's attitude puzzling him. "You doing what my wife wants you to do, I'll take as a personal favor to me. Now I'll find Royer myself."

He turned away, not seeing the grief in Derksen's childlike eyes. Ignoring Telfair and brushing Morehouse aside, he left the bank.

2

Darlington's was full. The crowd, in town for the evening's fights, was warming up before the contests would begin.

Gale pushed through the door and shouldered his way to the end of the bar where Darlington stood in his accustomed place, Cherry behind him.

Darlington said, "Good evening, Mr. Gale."

"Which is your head bartender?" said Gale.

"Why?"

"I'm looking for a man named Royer. Charley Royer. Know him?"

Darlington had been smoking. He removed his cheroot and stared thoughtfully at its glowing tip. "Seems like I've heard the name."

Behind him, Cherry drew a sharp, quick breath. She said to Gale, "What do you want with Royer?"

"He's interested in me," said Gale. "He took the trouble to shoot at me in the hills this afternoon. I want to know why."

Cherry looked at her brother, but Phil's full interest remained on his cigar. Her voice was bitter as she said, "No one can be trusted any more." Then she stepped around to face Gale.

"You'll find Royer at the fights. He's serving as one of Yankee Sullivan's seconds. But be careful of him, Ward. Watch him."

"I'll watch him," said Gale. He looked at her, curiously, then left the place.

Darlington started to move after him and Cherry stopped her brother with a word. "Phil!"

"What?" he said, pausing, but not looking back.

"Come here a minute, Phil. I want to talk to you."

"There's nothing to talk about," he said.

"Turn around, Phil," she said. "There's a lot to talk about."

He turned, unwillingly.

"You lied to me, Phil. It isn't so much that you sent Royer after Gale. It's that you sent him after you promised me you wouldn't. You're always talking about degrading me because you run this place. You're always talking about the slights I receive from the women on the other side of Washington. I don't mind those. I didn't mind anything, as long as I could trust you. But now that I can't, I have nothing left."

"Cherry," he said, and there was deep feeling in his voice. "Cherry, darling. The man's married."

"I'm twenty-three years old, Phil. There are certain things I have to decide for myself."

"No," he said. "I'm your brother. I'll decide."

She slapped him then, hard and sharp and final. While he stood there in the suddenly still saloon, she told him in a low, tense voice, "We're on one side or the other, Phil. I'm on Ward Gale's side. Make up your mind." Turning then she moved into the gambling room and climbed the stairs to their quarters above.

When she was gone Darlington moved toward the front door. Pushing the bat wings aside he came face to face with Gale.

"Mr. Gale," he said startled, and sought the proper words, not finding them. "My sister is a wonderful woman, as good as they come."

"She is," said Gale, and studied Darlington carefully. "It's too bad. Thank her for me and don't follow me any further." He moved on down Washington then, certain the gambler would not trail him.

The arena lay in a natural fold in the hills, its steeply rising sides making a small amphitheater. In the center was the squared ring and to the side the bear and bull pit. Already the crowd was gathering. Men sat in rising tiers about the central place. The sputtering knot torches and the burning tar barrels gave a reddish, smokish flare which threw their faces into unnatural relief.

Gale pressed through the crowd, pausing behind the group around Yankee Sullivan, and said to a miner on his right, "Which is Charley Royer?"

The miner pointed to a heavy set, paunchy man and Gale

pushed on toward him. Behind him the miner called out, trying to be of help, "Hey, Charley. Fellow wants to see you."

Royer turned. Across the heads of the packed crowd he saw Gale. For an instant he hesitated and Gale thought the man was reaching for a gun. Then Royer whirled and ran, diving through the crowd. Gale rushed him.

They panted up the hill, a dozen yards apart, Royer heading for the close-packed buildings of the Concho. Royer ducked into the first narrow alley. Gale came up to the dark slot and plunged in. In full flight, he hit Royer's outthrust boot before he saw the man. He went down skidding on his face.

Royer was over him like a cat, driving his heavy boot into the side of Gale's head. A thousand light splinters exploded in the air but Gale dragged himself upward despite the blinding pain, trying to see Royer and expecting another blow.

But Royer was running again, not having the nerve to stay at close quarters; Charley was the type who liked to play it safe. He knew the Concho well and he counted on his knowledge of the twisting alleyways to escape. He had a hundred yard start by the time Gale had gained his feet and started out again.

The alleys were unpaved, rutted from the recent rains, still muddy in spots. The only light came from a thin rind of moon hanging in the dark sky. Shadowy figures lurked in the doorways. Spanish voices called as he raced past. At one intersection he ran squarely into a Chinese and felt the man's coiled queue break loose and whip across his face. But always, somehow, he managed to keep Royer's fleeing figure in sight.

Gale's breath was growing short now and that kick in the head had done him no good, but Royer, too, was already faltering, worn down by the dogged pursuit. But as physical weariness overcame them and the pace slowed, Gale became conscious that he was now the middle man in this chase. Someone followed fast, but there was no time to look around without risking losing sight of Charley Royer.

Royer came to the far edge of the Concho and hesitated

for an instant, then swung into the alley which led down past Darlington's. Gale reached the corner in time to see Royer dart through the saloon's side door and thinking the man meant to come out the front onto Washington, he increased his speed and sprinted around the corner, hoping to head him off.

Coming up to the front entrance he slowed to a walk and peered in above the bat wing doors. The saloon was almost deserted, the crowd having departed for the fights. Only one bartender worked. A few customers loitered at the gaming tables. Darlington, his back to Gale, moved slowly toward the rear of the bar. Royer advanced toward him and behind the man came Cherry, her fists clenched.

Royer said, panting, "You got to help me, Phil. He's on my heels. He'll kill me."

"Who?" said Darlington. "And what have I got to do with it?"

"You sent me," said Royer, desperately. "You hired me."

"You're crazy," said Darlington. "I don't even know what you're talking about. Get out of here."

"Wait," said Cherry. "I want to talk with him, Phil."

Gale pushed in the front door. Royer saw him and yelled and bolted for the side door. "Jerry!" he shouted. "Frank! Help me."

Two players turned from a table, kicking back their chairs. Gale sprinted past them. He caught Royer at the doorway, his rush driving them out into the dark alley, his arms around the man's shoulders.

They went down together, rolling across the rutted mud to come up with a crash against the opposite building wall. Gale's big hands found Royer's throat and he tried to get to his knees. Two heavy bodies hit him then, flattening him across Royer and he knew the gamblers had joined the fight.

He tried to roll free, but these newcomers were fresh. A boot drove into his ribs. A pair of hands came over his shoulders to find his throat. He was hauled back from Royer and a fist drove hard into his face. He felt the strength run out of him.

Dimly he heard a crash and a man yell. The crash came again and the hands were gone from his throat. Freed, he

sensed Royer trying to crawl away and dropped on him.
Derksen's voice was at his ear.

"Larkin's coming, Mr. Gale. You'll be all right now."

3

Larkin, the marshal, was young, but already white of hair.
A coldly efficient man, he stayed behind Royer, prodding
him with his gun while he talked to Gale.

"You got any witnesses, Mr. Gale? I can't just take your
word he tried to kill you."

"I have a witness," said Gale. "I'll tell you who he is in
the morning. Just lock Royer up tonight."

"I can't do that," said Larkin.

"Yes you can," said Cherry. She stood in the doorway
across the alley from where she had witnessed the fight. "Go
ahead, Les. Lock him up. You can take my word for it."

Larkin hesitated, looking over Cherry's shoulder at Darlington. In this town there was a balance of power. Roberts directed things west of Washington, Darlington ruled
the Concho. "How about it, Phil?"

Darlington's voice was sharper than Gale had ever heard
it. "Don't ever doubt my sister's word, Les. Lock him up."

"All right," said Larkin, not pleased by the way Darlington had spoken. "Come on, Charley." He pushed his pris-
oner ahead of him across Washington.

Cherry spoke to Gale. "You going home now, Ward?"

"No," said Gale.

"You better come in then," she said. "You're a little battered. I'll fix you up."

"Cherry!" said Darlington.

"Come on, Ward," urged Cherry. "Please."

Gale moved slowly toward the door. Cherry reached out
and took his hand and Darlington stepped reluctantly aside
to let them pass. He watched them cross the gambling
room and mount the stairs.

In the living room above, Cherry gave Gale a drink, then
brought a basin of warm water.

"You're not very smart," she told Gale. "A smart man
wouldn't follow Charley Royer through the Concho."

"I got him," said Gale.

"They almost got you. They would have if it hadn't been for Ben Derksen. It's nice to have friends like that, Ward. Friends that want to help you."

Gale looked at her thoughtfully, realizing how beautiful she was. There was none of the hardness about her a man might expect to see. This, he thought, was to Darlington's credit. Then remembering how Prudence had turned on him, how cool Ben Derksen had been and how Spencer Morehouse had seemed to favor Telfair, he grew a little bitter.

"You're wrong, Cherry. I haven't any friends."

She laughed at him, slow and easy and musical. "Gale, Gale. You men are all alike. A woman turns against you and you haven't any friends."

He was startled, looking at her. "How did you know that Prudence . . ." he stopped, but Cherry had already picked it up, still laughing.

"I didn't, not until you said what you did about friends. Then you sounded so bitter. What's the matter, is she talking to Matt Roberts too much?"

"Either you have second sight, or spies." He was somewhat embarrassed.

"Neither," she said. "This is a small town, Ward, and I am not quite a part of it. Last year, the year before, there were almost no women in these hills. Then anyone in a dress was considered a lady. Times have changed. My brother operates a saloon. I sit in it. I drink with the customers, and sometimes when they please me—which is seldom—I invite them up here."

He flushed a little.

"I belong on this side of Washington," her tone was bitter. "But I can see across the square. You'd be surprised how much I know about the town, and the people in it."

He was silent, and she considered him. "You see," she said, "I can feel sorry for myself too."

He looked at her, at her dark beauty and sparkling eyes, at the low cut of her dress, so low that it showed the rounded fullness of her breasts.

"There's no reason for you to be lonely," he told her.

"No," she conceded. "There's no reason for me to be lonely, not in this country at least. A hundred miners have tried to sleep with me, fifty of them have been so interested that they offered marriage."

"And you turned them down." Gale was finding it much easier to talk to this girl than it had ever been for him to talk to Prudence.

"And I turned them down," she said. "Some of them had well-lined pokes. Some of them could have come close to buying Matt Roberts."

He laughed. "And it certainly is not money that you want from me for I haven't any."

"No," she said, and she came over to sit beside him. "It isn't money."

"And it isn't marriage, since I am already married."

"That I regret," she was entirely frank. "But you aren't happy in the marriage."

"My fault," he was quick to tell her.

"Probably," she said, "and I like you better for it. Most men have dismal tales of being misunderstood by their wives."

"Then what do you want?"

"You can start," she said, "by kissing me. After that, can't we let nature take its course?"

He laughed again and put his arm around her slender body and pulled her to him, and her mouth was hot and wet and demanding against his lips as she kissed him with her tongue.

His hand slipped up to her neck and down under the edge of her dress. He felt her shiver as his long fingers caressed the warm, pink-tipped mounds of her breasts and for an instant the room was a swinging dancing thing, for his senses were reeling.

Her lips were against his, pleading with him wordlessly. Suddenly, he never knew afterwards what happened, he pushed her from him and stood up.

For an instant Cherry stared up at him in amazement, then slowly anger gathered in her dark eyes. "So I'm not good enough for you, Ward Gale?"

He dropped to his knees then, and buried his head in her lap. "Please Cherry. It's not that."

"You've had other women," she said, and there was still a note of disbelief in her voice. "You must have."

"I have," he muttered.

"And I'm not good enough."

"You're too good," he said. "That's it, Cherry. You treat yourself too cheaply. With your looks, and your brains and your honesty you could be anything you chose. I've ruined one woman's life by lying. I'll be damned if I'll ruin yours."

She ran her fingers through his thick, coarse hair. "You do love her a great deal."

"I guess so," said Gale. "I seem to be all mixed up."

He straightened and she rose with him. "Kiss me once for luck, Ward."

He took her in his arms and held her closely thinking, Why not? Why not? Prudence is through with me. Prudence wouldn't even care. I could enjoy this. I could forget some of the things that worry me, and Cherry would be pleased. But instead he pushed her gently away, and she walked with him toward the door.

"You're the first man who ever repulsed me, Ward. Remember that."

"I didn't repulse you," he said gently. "It just wouldn't have worked for either of us."

She nodded. "You're right. I know you're right, yet even now I'm tempted to hold you."

"Hold me?" he was surprised. "How could you hold me?"

She laughed up at him. "Because of things I know," she said. "That banker of yours, your precious Mr. Telfair?"

"Telfair? What about him?"

"He's no more banker than I am. I saw him in San Francisco last year. He's a shoe salesman. Just remember that I know, that I might change my mind and want you still. If I send for you, remember that a word from me and your whole plan is ruined."

4

Leaving Darlington's, Gale crossed Washington and walked slowly past the Holbrook House, then the jail and on to the water company office. As he passed the jail he saw

Larkin seated on the old desk, his hat drawn well down over his eyes.

In the building next door, a single light burned. Ben Derksen sat at the desk, the shotgun lying beside his arm, the sawed off barrels pointed directly at the doorway. He caught up the gun and raised it automatically as Gale came in.

"Why you should sing out before you walk up on a man," Ben said.

Gale smiled faintly. "Not much danger of anyone walking up on you, Ben. I want to thank you for what you did in the alley. What changed your mind?"

Derksen looked down at his bulging stomach. "Why I guess I got to figuring. If they'd have done for you, you couldn't have built the water ditch for her."

"Was that the only reason, Ben?"

Derksen shifted, uncomfortably. "Mr. Gale, I just don't understand. It's seldom I like a man right off. But that day in Stockton, when you licked Chauncey Burns, I liked you right off. And then for you to do a thing like that."

"Like what, Ben?"

"Like marrying a decent girl, just to get even with Roberts. That's a low thing to do. If you'd only loved her."

"Ben," said Gale, startled, "What do you know about that? What makes you think I don't love her?"

"Why I guess if you loved her, she'd know it, wouldn't she?"

Gale shook his head. "Sometimes, when you get hurt, you can't see things. But I do love her. I know now, I've loved her all the time. I don't know what happened. When I came back from the hills, she had changed. Someone must have told her something. I don't think Roberts could have convinced her. Maybe it was Morehouse. You can't tell what Spencer will do, or why."

"It wasn't Spencer told her," said Ben.

"It doesn't make any difference now," said Gale, wearily. "The damage is done. She's been hurt. All I can do now is build her the water ditch. When that's done, I'll find the man who told her."

"I guess you will," said Ben. "And I guess maybe you'll make him pay for it."

"Yes," said Gale. "But right now we have a ditch to build. I'll need the money, Ben."

"What money?"

"The money in the box. I'm going to borrow it for the water company. You're not going to try and stop me, are you?"

Derksen thought this over. "Why Mr. Gale," he said, "when you were in here earlier, you said Mr. Telfair wasn't a banker. Is that right?"

"That's right," said Gale.

Ben scratched his head. "It beats all. I don't know whether I'm coming or going. Time was, when a man said something, you could believe it. Now . . ." He stared helpless at Gale, his simple, direct mind confused by the devious forces pressing in upon him.

"Listen, Ben," said Gale. "Can you believe this? I'm not stealing this money. I'm borrowing it to build the ditch. The water company will give the bank stock to secure the loan. As soon as the ditch is finished, everyone will want to buy stock in it. The bank can then sell the shares they are holding and recover their deposits. Or they can hold them and draw interest on the loan. You understand that?"

"Why I guess that sounds honest enough," said Ben.

Gale said, "It isn't honest, Ben. It would only be honest if the bank, itself, had some capital of its own to make the loan. This bank has no capital. Its deposits we're going to take. But, by completing the ditch, we help the depositors to help themselves."

"You lost me there," said Derksen. "But if you say we should, we'll do it. A man's got to trust somebody. When do you want the money?"

"Now," said Gale. "I'll go down and talk to Emil Aruup. He's the biggest merchant in Carolina. He knows more about where to lay his hands on supplies than anyone else in the country. If he agrees, we'll carry the money down to his safe. But Ben, don't mention this loan to anyone, except Morehouse and Telfair. If you do, the whole thing's ruined."

"Me," said Ben, "I guess I've talked too much already. I won't say anything."

Aruup was smoking his late pipe when Gale came in. Gale

said, "I'd like to talk to you. Are you about ready to close up?"

The merchant was a silent man. He made his way across the cluttered floor between the coils of rope and stacked shovels and barred the front door. Then he led Gale to the living quarters in the rear. "What's on your mind?"

Gale said, "We're ready to start building the ditch. We have a hundred thousand dollars, which I want to hand to you tonight. I'll tell you roughly what we need. Enough timber for eight miles of flume. Iron braces to hang it to two miles of canyon wall. Logs for a dam and trestles. Tools to work with. Powder. And enough labor to complete the job."

"Why come to me?" said Aruup.

"Because you know this country. You know where the materials can be found."

Aruup knocked out the heel of his pipe. "You must think I'm a damned fool, Gale. The minute I started, Roberts would be on my neck from morning until night. And if you failed to complete the ditch, I'd be ruined. And you haven't got a chance in the world. You need any help bringing the money here?"

"No," said Gale, and grasped the man's hand.

He and Derksen made a dozen trips. When the last of the dust had been transfered to Aruup's big safe, the three of them sat down, Aruup with pen and paper before him. Derksen proved surprisingly helpful. Having worked on the Roberts' flume, Ben had retained in his mind every detail of construction.

They would bring in a saw mill first, setting it up above the dam site and cut four inch puncheons for the walls and flooring of the flume. The iron would have to come from Stanford's store in Sacramento. The tools Aruup would purchase in San Francisco. Between them, Aruup and Derksen named a dozen men who had building experience in the East and who would serve as foremen on various sections of the ditch, for it was no part of their plans to wait until the dam was completed. This had to be done hurriedly if they hoped to fill their basin before the snows melted in the high hills and the rivers ran low.

Morning customers had already banged on Aruup's front

door before they finished. The merchant cooked them a late breakfast and, after they finished eating, Gale and Ben stepped out into the street. As they approached the water company office, Morehouse and Telfair came out of the Holbrook House and turned toward them, both men unconsciously hurrying when they saw Ben.

"What's the idea, Ben?" Telfair said angrily. "Why aren't you in there guarding the money? That's what we hired you for."

"Why," said Derksen, "everything's safe enough. There's no money to guard. Mr. Gale borrowed all of it."

"Borrowed it!" Telfair turned white, then said angrily to Gale, "By God you won't get away with this."

"You better keep your voice low, Mister," said Gale. "If anyone hears you yelling about lending all your money, he might want his deposit back. And then where would you be?"

Telfair glanced around and wiped his forehead with the sleeve of his coat. "Let's go into the office and talk this thing over."

"There's nothing to talk about," said Gale. "I'm tired. I've been working all night spending that money. Spencer's the business man of the water company. Get him to make out enough shares of stock to cover the loan. And by the way, we'll need more money from time to time. You better get some more deposits."

"You'll play hell getting it," said Telfair.

"We'll get it," Gale said. "Until that water ditch is finished, your bank is in bad shape, Mr. Rothschild. You better turn all your efforts to help us. That's your only chance."

"Damn you," said Morehouse. "I've got a good notion to. . . ."

"To do what?" said Gale.

In the interval they appraised each other, Morehouse lost his angry look. "That's just it, Ward. What the hell can I do?" He turned to Telfair, letting himself enjoy the other's discomfort. "Just when you think you've got Gale in a corner, he turns the tables on you. The only chance any of us have now, is to finish the damned ditch. I never thought I'd live to see the day when I would work on something this big for nothing."

"That's all fine," said Telfair. "But what happens? The first customer into the bank is going to see that the packing case is empty."

"No," said Morehouse, dryly. "We can't let that happen. Use your head." He turned to Ben Derksen. "Fill up those empty money sacks with gravel and stack them in the case. It will be your job to see no one gets close enough to that case to find out the difference."

"I don't care what you do," said Gale. "I'm going to bed. I'll use your room, Spence, so I'll be handy. No use of me going all the way home."

Without waiting for an answer he started for the Holbrook House. As he came opposite the jail, the marshal rushed out, almost running into him.

"Damn them," he said, "they can't do that to my jail."

Gale stopped. "Can't do what?"

"They dug a hole through the rear wall."

"Who did?"

"Charley's friends. He's gone." Then really looking at Gale for the first time, he said, "You better watch yourself. Charley was awful mad. He didn't think you played fair with him, having him put in jail that way."

9.

WITH THE DITCH STARTED, Kellogg was happy. One of his
two dreams was coming true under the impetus of the big
redhead who had become his son-in-law. His second dream,
that of making Carolina the capital of California, was bound
to follow. The petitions with their forty thousand names
were piled neatly on his library shelves. All that was necessary now was to wait until the fall session of the legislature
and present them.

The speed with which the water ditch progressed surprised even Gale. Emil Aruup, under his quiet, dry exterior,
had proven to be an intense, driving man. The mountains of
material grew. The saw mill was already spewing out timbers
cut from soft sugar pine. The lower cribbing for the dam
was in. Men suspended by swaying ropes drilled holes into
the rock face of the canyon wall and fastened the iron
brackets into place.

Four crews worked at timbering for the trestles and the
building of these went forward under Gale's personal direction. But Aruup's purchases and the steady drain of labor's
wages ate huge holes in the store of money and Gale was
forced to call on Telfair again and again. Fortunately, the
miners' confidence in the Rothschild Bank increased and
the deposits mounted steadily. But no matter how they
grew, Gale syphoned them off as the wearying days turned
into weeks, the weeks into months.

When necessity forced him into Carolina, which was

often, since he had to keep in constant touch with Aruup, Telfair and Morehouse, Gale stayed at the Kellogg place as Prudence demanded. When her father was present, Prudence was gay and interested, demanding that Gale tell her of the full progress of the work. But when they were alone in the confines of their room, she never spoke to him.

It was a curious arrangement and one Gale could have easily made intolerable for her, but he made no effort to cross the invisible boundary she had drawn, thus making it intolerable for himself.

Occasionally, in the forgetfulness of sleep, her arm came out to circle him and he would lie there in the darkness miserable and lonely. There was only one thing he had to be thankful for. Since that first night he had come home from the hills, Roberts had never come back to the Kellogg house. Whether that decision had been made by Roberts or Prudence, he had no way of knowing and he would not ask.

Three times Gale had been shot at from the brush. Whether this was Roberts' work or Charley Royer, or Chauncey Burns attempting to settle old scores, Gale did not know. But he did know the planned attacks on the working crews could stem from no other source than Roberts. Men had been waylaid and killed. One trestle had been fired and destroyed, forcing them to hire guards, which added to the expense and increased their difficulties. And there were open boasts in the saloons along Washington that Roberts would never let them make the crossing of his right-of-way.

Cherry Darlington added to Gale's worries. Three times she had sent messages to him demanding he come to see her. The third had been delivered to the bank and Morehouse looked at him questioningly.

"She's a lot of woman, Ward. Haven't women caused you enough trouble already?"

Gale flared at him. "What do you know about my troubles, Spence?"

"I'm not a fool," said Morehouse. "I'm not deceived by appearances."

"You're a fool if you think I'm interested in Cherry Darlington," said Gale. "I'm only interested in one woman."

Morehouse's eyes were bright and probing. "Then why do

you spend so much time at Darlington's? If you don't go there yourself, she sends for you. And you do what she says. And look, Ward, I'm not the only one who's noticing that. Wilson Kellogg's no fool, either. In a town this size, you can't get by with a thing like this."

Gale said, angrily, "I'm not trying to get by with anything, Spence. If you want to know the truth, I go to see Cherry Darlington because I have to. Cherry knows Telfair isn't a banker. One word from her and you'd see a run on the bank. The only reason she hasn't told her brother, so far, is that I go to see her."

"My God!" said Morehouse. "Why didn't you tell me this before?"

"Because, said Gale, "if I had, Telfair would have folded up and run out and you would have been useless to me."

"But Ward. What if she gets serious? We better do something."

"Sure," said Gale. "We better do something. Because when I've got enough money out of this bank to complete the work, I won't go to see her any more. Compared to Prudence, I don't care what happens to Telfair, or you, or me, or Matt Roberts. You're a smart man, Spence. You better figure out a way to get her off my neck."

For a moment Morehouse let his guard fall and Gale saw something he had never seen before. "I'd like to," the small man said. "And Ward, you're not good for Cherry. Maybe that's what I've been worrying about, you going over there so often. Maybe I should do something about it." He rose, straightened his coat and, without another word, left the bank. Through the window, Gale watched him cross to Darlington's.

2

The dam was done. Behind the earth-filled walls the lake began to form. The hanging portion of the flume was in place and carefully guarded. The trestles were completed. All that remained now was four miles of gravity flow ditch and the crossing of Matt Roberts' flume.

They held a conference in the bank. Gale, Morehouse,

Telfair and Wilson Kellogg. Gale said, "It will only take forty thousand more. That's what Aruup figures. We've got to have the money. Otherwise, everything we've done is lost."

Telfair had been pacing the floor. Derksen sat in his accustomed place on the packing case. The banker swung around, running long fingers nervously through his hair.

"But Ward, what you ask is impossible. Our withdrawals are almost as big as our new deposits now. This camp is old enough so that many men have made their pile and are heading home. We have thirty-five thousand dollars on hand. Our books show that we have better than two hundred and fifty thousand dollars on deposit. The difference has been loaned to your water company. What would happen if we had a small run? Suppose there was a new strike? Suppose a lot of men wanted to leave fast? What would happen then?"

"Things haven't changed," said Gale. "Let me have thirty thousand."

"No."

"Let me have twenty."

"No."

"My dear sir," said Wilson Kellogg. "Mr. Gale has done everything humanly possible. You have to stand behind him now. Why can't you send word to your principals and explain the situation? Surely they're not going to throw over two hundred thousand dollars for the lack of thirty more."

Gale, Morehouse and Telfair looked at each other. It was up to Telfair. He stood with his head down for a moment, thinking. When he looked up he spoke to Kellogg, but his sly smile was for Gale.

"All I can do, Mr. Kellogg, is to send a dispatch out on the morning stage. It will take time to receive the answer. Naturally, we will have to hold up the work until it arrives." He brushed his hands. "I guess that settles it, Mr. Gale."

Gale kept his anger to himself and stood up. With Kellogg present there was nothing further he could say. "It's late, Wilson," he said. "Let's go home."

"Yes," said Kellogg. "First thing in the morning I must leave for Sonora to welcome the Governor. He is to be the guest of honor at the *baille*. And, gentlemen," he paused and rubbed his palms together, "I shall speak to him about making Carolina the capital. My petitions are all ready."

They walked down Silver in silence. Not until they made the turn onto Adams did Kellogg speak.

"Ward," he said then, "what's the matter?"

"We're licked," said Gale. "If we don't get some more money, I can't pay the crews next week."

"I wasn't thinking about the ditch. I was thinking about you and Prudence and the Darlington woman."

Gale stopped dead, searching for an answer. Kellogg continued, "I have watched Prudence when she thought herself not observed. She's unhappy. I told you that morning, at Simmons' Tent, that if you ever let my daughter down, I'd kill you. You had better watch yourself, Ward."

Coming into the house, Ward found that Prudence had already gone upstairs. He climbed to their room, pushed open the door and found her already in bed, her face turned away from him. He shut the door quietly and moved over to stand beside her.

"Prudence," he said, "we have to have a talk."

She did not move, but he knew she was awake. "You made the rules and they've been hard to keep. But your father spoke to me tonight. This thing has gotten away from us. We can't go on this way. I'm not blaming you. I'm saying only that it isn't fair to drag your father into our misery. I'm going out for a walk now. I want to think things over. While I'm gone, you do the same. There are two choices. Either you can believe me when I tell you that I love you, or we separate. If we do that, as soon as I complete this ditch, I'll leave Carolina."

"Where will you go to do your thinking?" she asked. "Darlington's?"

"I could," he said. "I'm welcome there." With that he left her.

But he did not go to Darlington's. Nor was there anything for him to think about. The decision was up to Prudence.

It was over an hour later when he came out on the ridge above Roberts' flume and stood looking down at the point where the two ditches had to cross. Here a fire burned, sending out its small light against the circle of darkness, showing him the armed guards Roberts had placed there to prevent the crossing.

He wasted ten minutes watching them and planning his campaign, then moved slowly back toward town. Later he passed the Kellogg house. The place was dark. He went on to the Square, surprised at the few lights showing; he had not been conscious of the passing time. Still sleepless, he moved into the Square and, pausing beside the bandstand, he put his back against the rough bark of the Hangman's Oak and lit a cigar.

After two puffs, the tobacco tasted stale and he threw it away, the coal making a shower of sparks as it struck the dry packed earth. Then, still dissatisfied, he crossed Silver and entered the Holbrook House.

There was no one in the lobby. He rounded the high desk and lifted a key from the board. Upstairs, he let himself into an empty room. Without making a light, he sat down on the edge of the bed. Then it was he heard the sharp clout of a single pistol shot.

3

Matt Roberts, with Allison beside him, sat in the darkened express building watching the conference that went on behind the lighted windows of the water company office.

"They're up to something," Roberts said.

Allison's dry voice answered. "There's rumors among the workmen that they're getting short of money. They've already laid off some of the crews."

"Rothschilds running out of money?" said Roberts.

"We don't know it is the Rothschilds yet, do we?" said Allison. "Unless you've had some word you haven't told me about."

"I've had no answer." Roberts sounded dissatisfied. "But we can't wait any longer. They're ready to make their crossing. All they have to do then is dig a ditch into town. We've got to stop them."

"If it isn't the Rothschilds," said Allison, "where are they getting the money?"

"I don't know," said Roberts. "Unless they're using the deposits of the new bank. As near as I can figure from talking with the man who sold Aruup materials, they must have spent in the neighborhood of two hundred thousand already. It's hard to believe that a new bank would have taken in that much in deposits."

"They've taken most of our business," said Allison, glumly. "I've expected you to do something about it, Matt. When you come right down to cases, this is all Ward Gale's doing. The man's rubbed it into you and you've taken it."

"You've run my business well, Geoffry," said Roberts. "But I'm perfectly capable of running my own personal life. When the right cards turn up, I'll play them, but I have to know what the game is first."

"You'll never know unless one of them talks," said Allison.

Roberts looked speculatively across the Square. The meeting was breaking up. He watched Kellogg and Gale leave together and saw Morehouse and Telfair turn in the opposite direction. The banker swung into the Holbrook House. Morehouse continued on across Washington and disappeared into Darlington's. Both Allison and Roberts noted this and Allison said, in a dissatisfied voice, "Morehouse seems to have found a new interest."

Roberts glanced at him sideways. "First Gale and then Morehouse," he said. "You don't like that one little bit, do you Geoffry?"

"She's too good for that place," said Allison. "She's too good." He spoke almost to himself.

Roberts made an impatient gesture and glanced back toward the water company office where Derksen was putting out the window lights. "Ben used to like to drink, didn't he?"

"What's that?" said Allison, his mind still across Washington.

"I said Derksen likes to drink. And he's been present at all their conferences. He knows where they got the money. And he's a simple minded fool. Take a bottle over there and see what you can find out."

"I'd rather not," said Allison.

"I don't care what you'd rather not," said Roberts. "I'll

be in my rooms when you get through. Get the hog drunk and find out what he knows."

He got up then and moved out onto the street, leaving Allison alone. The banker sat there, resenting Roberts' order. He found it distasteful, and he found it more distasteful that he could not find the courage to disobey. He rose at last and started the precise pattern of his ways. He circled the Square at the corners, pausing only in the saloon next to Darlington's to buy a bottle of whisky.

Derksen was surprised to see him coming through the door. "Why Mr. Allison," he said.

"I was passing," said Allison. "How are things?"

"Why all right," said Derksen. "They're fine."

"It's a nice night," said Allison. "I couldn't sleep and was taking a walk."

Derksen eyed the bottle the man carried. "Taking that home to a friend, was you?"

"A friend? Oh." Allison laughed in his dry way. "That's a good one, Ben. As a matter of fact, I like to keep a bottle in my room. I was all out. Would you like a drink?"

"Well now," said Derksen, "I don't know as it would be polite to refuse."

He accepted the bottle and started the cork, then opening the drawer of Spencer's desk, produced two glasses, pouring generously. He offered one of the tumblers to Allison. "Here's how?" he said, and drained his glass.

Allison had to empty his. He would have liked to wait awhile, but Ben poured again.

"You know, Geoffry," said Ben, "we should be better acquainted. We're both in the banking business, as the fellow says. Both of us working for somebody else and them making all the money."

Allison's mouth tightened. "That's right, Ben. And what do we get out of it?"

"Callouses," said Ben. "Drink up, Geoffry. It won't be this way all the time. How's your bank doing since mine started up?"

Allison drank again and felt the whisky run through him with warming fingers. His resentment against Roberts was a growing thing. He looked across the desk at the slovenly fat man and thought, this is a poor occupation for a gentleman, trying to worm information out of a drunkard. Derksen, un-obtrusively, refilled both glasses.

"It must be nice," said Allison, "working for people like the Rothschilds."

"Huh," said Derksen. "What do I get out of it? What do you get out of your bank?"

"My salary," said Allison.

"It ain't enough," said Derksen. "All good bankers should get interest. Hey, you ain't drinking up."

Allison had lost count of his drinks. He emptied the glass. In all of his careful life he had never felt this way before.

"Ben," he said, his voice slightly thickened, "I'm curious. How do the Rothschilds get their money into this bank? It didn't come in by the express."

Derksen shook his head laboriously. "I tell you, Geof, these here Rothschilds have got a lot of banks. They're plumb all over the place. Now if men was to know how they shifted their money here and there, they'd lose a lot of it. So they keep it a secret. I ain't supposed to tell." He filled the glasses again.

Allison steadied himself as he picked up the drink. "Ben," he said, "as one banker to another, that would be a good thing to know. Maybe you and I might have a bank of our own, someday. How do they do it?"

Ben looked cautiously around the gloomy room. Then he filled the glasses again, thrusting one into Allison's hand. He put his big arm around Allison's shoulder and drew him close. "Geof," he whispered, "I don't know. That's the trouble with foreigners. They don't tell a man nothing. All I know is, that when I come at night, there's always a new shipment in. Maybe they make it some place out in the hills."

He sat down heavily and let his head fall slowly down upon his crossed arms. Allison stared blearily at him for a moment, then had some difficulty hitting the front door squarely. Once on the street, he hesitated, finally turning toward Darlington's.

When he had gone, Derksen straightened. An inch of fluid remained in the bottom of the whisky bottle. He drained it at a gulp, then walking steadily, he went to the door and pitched the empty bottle into the Square. Stand-

ing outside, he watched Allison move tipsily into Darlington's.

"Now what the hell," said Ben, cold sober, "did he want?"

4

Inside the saloon, Allison paused to orient himself, fo-
cusing his eyes with some difficulty. The place was only
medium filled, but look as he might he could see no sign of
Morehouse or Cherry and a cold anger came up to partially
clear the fog from his brain.

He saw Darlington at the end of the bar and moved toward him. The gambler said, "Good evening, Mr. Allison,"
and gave him a studied look. "You're a little late."

"That's my business," said Allison and brushed on past
the man, mumbling, "I want to see that no good sister of
yours."

"Allison!" said Darlington, sharply, "don't ever. . . ."

Allison paid no attention. In the rear gambling room he
paused beside a roulette table and looked at the stairway
leading to the rooms above. He would have liked to climb
them and he wished he were man enough to make the try.
But the best he could do was let his imagination run wild.
*Cherry and Morehouse. Cherry and Morehouse. Cherry and
Morehouse.* It beat a rhythm into his unsteady mind.

"Make your bets, gentlemen," the roulette dealer said.

The words broke through the fever of Allison's thoughts.
He turned, staring at the gambling table as if he had never
seen it before. That was it. Make a bet. Make a big splash.
That's what women liked, a man who made a big splash.
A man who took his chances. A man who won. Why a man
could even win this place from Darlington. That would
bring her to him.

Although he spent grudgingly, Geoffry Allison always
carried considerable money with him. He had a deep fear
of poverty and the knowledge that his pockets were well
lined, bolstered his ego. But now, he was drunk.

"Five hundred dollars on the red," he said, pulling the
money from his pockets.

The wheel turned and the white ball whirred around the

upper rim, spun by the dealer's supple fingers. Allison could not follow it. It slowed, finally, dropping down, bouncing twice and settling into Number Sixteen. He had won.

He won again and yet again. The stack of gold before him grew, and this was more intoxicating than the whisky fumes rising in his brain. Men circled the table, drawn by his large play and for the first time in his life, Allison savored the heady uplift of jovial attention. These men were his friends. They were pulling for him. They wanted him to win. He was winning. He wondered how Darlington felt. He wondered how the dealer felt. That man's face was impassive.

Allison felt himself thinking clearer now. He'd been a fool. It was simple arithmetic that if he had bet twice as much he would have won twice as much. He increased his bets. Sometimes he won and sometimes he lost. It was difficult to keep track. But suddenly the gold which had been piled before him was gone. He had enough left for one more bet.

Sweat broke out across his forehead and he used a white handkerchief to wipe it away. No longer conscious of the crowd pressing about him, he was only aware of the spinning wheel. He made the bet and standing, his hands gripped at his sides, watched the ivory ball. He lost.

Blindly he turned away and ran directly into Darlington. The gambler's mouth was coldly cynical, his eyes hard and filled with deep dislike.

"You're not stopping now, Mr. Allison. Two bets and you'd be as far ahead as you were five minutes ago."

"I'm out of money," Allison muttered.

"Your credit's good," said Phil, and looked over at the dealer. "Let him have twenty thousand, Joe."

Allison turned back uncertainly. He stared at the gold the dealer pushed toward him. Its value had no meaning to him; he had won such large sums there for awhile. He could win again. Why not? He pushed five thousand onto the red.

"A bet," said the dealer and spun the wheel. The money lasted four plays.

When the realization of what had happened struck him, Allison was cold sober, shaking. He pushed his way through the crowd, not conscious that Darlington was at his heels, and half blindly felt his way along the bar.

"Wait," said Darlington.

Allison stopped. "What do you want?"

"This wasn't your lucky night," the gambler said. "When can I expect my twenty thousand?"

"Twenty thousand?" said Allison, the sum making sense to him for the first time. "Why I haven't got twenty thousand dollars, Phil. You knew that when you pressed it on me."

Darlington was relentless. "A man doesn't gamble when he can't pay. I want the money by morning or I'll send someone to collect."

Allison was frightened. "Now wait a minute, Phil. You can't do that. After all, we both work for Matt Roberts."

"I work for no one," said Darlington. "Twenty thousand by morning." He stood there and watched Allison leave the room, the banker more unsteady now than when he had come in.

5

When business was done, Darlington stepped out onto dark Washington Street. He was still angered by Allison's careless reference to Cherry. Baiting Allison into losing a fortune had not brought him the satisfaction he thought it would and pride called for him to make the man pay.

Seeing the lights still burning in Roberts' Bank, he moved like a shadow along the side street and peered through a crack in the partly drawn shades. Allison was seated at the desk, his head bowed into his hands.

For five minutes Darlington watched him, then making his decision, he turned to the Union Exchange at the end of the block and climbed the stairs to Roberts' room.

Roberts was not pleased to see him. Angrily he said, "You're not supposed to come here and you know it."

Darlington's pride had already suffered this night, but he took this added slur without changing expression. "No one saw me," he said. "It's very late. The lobby's empty."

Roberts was not appeased. "What do you want here, anyway?"

"I wanted to ask you," said Darlington, "if you'll guarantee the payment of the twenty thousand Allison lost to-night?"

Roberts started. "You mean he was gambling?"

"You can call it that," said Darlington. "He owes me twenty thousand. I've told him that I want it by morning."

"You're a fool to trust him," Roberts said. "He hasn't got twenty thousand dollars."

"He'll get it," said Darlington. "He's afraid of me. Right now he's sitting down in your bank thinking about it."

"Oh," said Roberts. "He is, is he?" Turning, he moved to his writing table, opened a drawer and lifted out a pistol. This he put in his belt. "Come on, Phil," he said.

They descended the stairs in silence, stepping out of the front door into the shadow of the overhead gallery. As they did so, both of them saw Gale round the corner off of Adams and walk slowly toward the bandstand in the Square.

Neither of them moved. They watched Gale stop and lean against the Hangman's Oak, saw the flare as he lighted his cigar, and then the small fountain of sparks as he hurled it away and moved over to enter the Holbrook House.

"Something's bothering him," Darlington said.

"Yes," said Roberts. "Maybe we can bother him some more. Come on."

Allison was no longer at the desk when they peered in. He was down on his knees. The door of the big safe was opened and Allison, surrounded by pokes, was pouring a small quantity of gold dust from each of the leather bags.

Roberts pushed open the door. Allison turned, his face whitening.

"Why Matt!" he said. "I. . . ."

Roberts shot him through the head.

Even Darlington was shocked, but Roberts was coolly unmoved. He pushed the gambler out of the building. "If you hope to collect that twenty thousand, Phil, you'll back up what I say." Then he was running lightly across the Square. Darlington followed him.

Larkin, rubbing sleep from his eyes, was just coming out of the jail when Roberts pushed him back inside.

"What was that?" said Larkin. "What was that shot?"

"Gale killed Allison," said Roberts.

"What?"

"That's right. Both Darlington and I saw it. Gale asked for an appointment tonight. I was too busy to see him. I told Allison to talk to him."

The marshal's face showed his surprise. "What did Gale want with you?"

"I don't know," said Roberts. "But I think his bank's in trouble. I think he hoped to get help from us. I can only guess. But I imagine that after he had told Allison his story and Geoffry refused to help, Gale lost his head and shot him."

The marshal was a careful man. He knew the inner working of the town. Roberts and Darlington represented both sides of Washington Street. Gale was an outsider.

"Phil," said Larkin, "did you see it?"

In the interval, before he answered, Darlington knew he held Carolina in the palm of his hand. His decision was colored by two things—his resentment at Cherry's interest in Gale and his love for money. Once he testified for Roberts, he was inexorably bound to the man. But if he told the truth, he would lose twenty thousand dollars and Gale would control Carolina. He made his bet.

"That's what happened," he said. "Allison was in my place. I walked out after him and he told me he had an appointment with Gale at the bank. After a while there was a shot and Gale ran out. I got there the same time Matt did. Gale ran across to Holbrook House. He threw the gun into the Square. It was Matt who thought to pick it up."

Larkin took the gun from Roberts' hand, making his decision. "All right," he said. "Let's go find Gale."

10.

SITTING on the edge of the bed, Gale heard the pound of boots rising on the stairs. Doors along the hall opened and closed. Sleepy voices protested angrily. Curiosity lifted him to his feet and he stepped out into the hallway, still fully dressed.

Larkin had almost reached his door. The marshal stopped, staring.

Gale said, "What's the excitement?"

"You," said Larkin. "I'm looking for you." He swung up his gun and pushed it against Gale's side. "Why did you kill Allison?"

"Allison?" said Gale. Behind the marshal he saw Roberts and Darlington. "What is this?"

Telfair came out of his room and seeing this, held back. But Spencer Morehouse pushed forward, jostling Larkin. "Have you lost your mind, Les?" Spencer said. "Who says Gale killed Allison?"

"Roberts and Darlington. They both saw him."

"Those two? Why wouldn't they say a thing like that?"

"Now wait a minute," said Larkin. He looked at Gale. "What have you got to say about this?"

"I hardly knew Allison," said Gale. "Start using your head, Larkin."

"I'm using it," said Larkin. "What are you doing here? Why are you all dressed up this time of night?"

"I came here to sleep," said Gale. "I just got here."

"That's a good one," said Larkin. "You with a house and a nice wife, so you come here to sleep." He put out a hand and touched Gale's shirt. "Warm and sweaty," Larkin went on. "You could have got that way running." He was now fully convinced.

"Listen," said Gale. "Don't you realize, that of all the men in camp, Roberts has the most to gain by doing this?"

"I'm not the alcalde," said Larkin. "You can tell him anything you want to, in the morning. Come on."

"Wait a minute," said Morehouse. "Maybe Gale doesn't want to go with you?" He looked at Gale, brightly.

"Keep out of it, Spencer," said Gale. "No use both of us being arrested. Get Kellogg down here." Gale moved out ahead of Larkin, not even bothering to glance at Roberts or Darlington.

In the jail office, Larkin indicated a cot in the corner. "I'll have to keep you in here. The back of the cell, where Charley broke out, hasn't been fixed yet. But don't try anything, Gale. It won't do you any good."

Gale stepped to the barred window that overlooked the Square. The thick branches of the Hangman's Oak stood out menacingly against the lightening sky. It was nearly morning and he turned back to the cot. "Mind if I sleep?"

He was barely settled down when Morehouse returned with Wilson Kellogg. Gale rose, looking past them for Prudence, but she did not appear.

Kellogg, seeing that look, said quickly, "I made her stay home, Ward. She's upset and I don't want her around now. This is serious."

"You got here quick enough," Gale said.

"I was ready to leave for Sonora," said Kellogg. "Another five minutes and I would have been gone." He turned to Larkin and his oratorical pompousness came back, and he was a lawyer again. "Now, sir, let's have the facts."

Larkin repeated Roberts' charge and Darlington's testimony. Kellogg chuckled, confident. "This is the most absurd thing I've ever heard. With me defending Mr. Gale, we'll laugh them out of town."

"I wouldn't be too sure," said Larkin, stubbornly. "I'm going to have a few things to say. For instance, why was

Gale at the Holbrook House instead of being at home with his wife?"

Kellogg turned slowly on Gale. "Yes, where were you last night, Ward?"

"I was walking in the hills," said Gale. "I couldn't sleep."

"No, Ward," said Cherry Darlington. She stood in the doorway, her hair loose about her shoulders, a scarlet wrapper drawn tight about her body, her small feet showing through the lacings of native sandals. "Tell them the truth. Tell them why you couldn't have killed Geoffry Allison. Tell them you were with me all the time. It makes no difference to me."

"No," said Gale. "How could I tell them that?"

"Then I'll tell them," she said. She looked at Larkin, then at Kellogg. "He was with me. I'll testify he was with me."

Kellogg's face whitened until the tight drawn skin across his cheekbones matched the color of his beard. Larkin was embarrassed and turned away.

"Cherry," said Morehouse, pleadingly. "You don't know what you're doing. This won't help and it isn't the truth."

Cherry moved her head and looked out at the Hangman's Oak. When she turned back she shuddered. "It is the truth," she said. "Who knows better than I do?"

"That's right, madam," said Wilson Kellogg. "Who should know better than you? But your testimony won't do any good." Without another word he left the office.

2

Larkin was in the middle of the Square helping to set up the tables for the alcalde's court which would convene at one o'clock. Gale, at the front window, was watching the groups of miners drifting into town when he saw Prudence moving toward the jail, along Silver.

Anticipation heartened him and he was shocked when she swerved, just short of the jail and cut over to the Square side of the street. Everyone turned to look at her. She was the center of interest, but she held her head high and spoke to no one.

Reaching Washington, she crossed the street and walked

deliberately into Darlington's Saloon. This stopped all activity in the Square.

A minute later the side door of Darlington's opened and Cherry appeared followed by Prudence. They stood face to face in the sunbaked alley, talking for a full five minutes. Then, without a backward glance, Prudence walked away from the Darlington girl and recrossed Washington.

This time she made no effort to avoid the jail, but came directly to the barred window and looked in on Gale. Her eyes were deep, dark pools in her drawn face and it hurt Gale to see the marks of grief there.

"Prudence," he said. "You shouldn't have done that."

"There are a lot of things that should never have been done," said Prudence. "But I had to talk to her."

"I wasn't with her last night," said Ward.

"I know it," said Prudence. "She told me. But she's going to swear, at the trial, that you were."

"I won't let her," said Gale.

"She'll do it anyway. She loves you, Ward. Do you love her? No . . . don't answer that." She spoke quickly before he had a chance to make his denial. "I had no right to ask that."

"You're my wife," he said. "You have every right."

"No. But don't worry, Ward. No matter what happens at the trial, I'll get you free. I think I've found a way."

"Don't do anything foolish," he said. "Not for me. I've caused too many people too much trouble, already. This will turn out all right. Your father will get me out of it."

There was pity in the look she gave him, then she was gone, hurrying.

"Prudence!" Gale called after her. "Prudence!" But she did not come back.

Gale was beside himself. Since Prudence had made the trip across Washington and the town had seen her talking to Cherry Darlington, he had to somehow prevent the gambler's sister from testifying. For five minutes he paced the jail office like a caged animal, coming back to the window again and again. Finally he saw Morehouse rushing along Silver and heard the little man shout.

"Larkin," said Morehouse. "I want into the jail. I have to see Gale."

The marshal came rumbling across the beaten ground, bringing out his keys as he walked. Still muttering, he unlocked the door. Morehouse brushed past him and Larkin stepped into the room.

Gale seized the little man's shoulder. "Spence, where's Prudence gone? What's she up to?"

"I don't know," said Morehouse. "I don't care. There's hell to pay. Kellogg's drunk. I tried to sober him up but I can't. He's stinking drunk. You know what that means, Ward? An hour after the trial, you'll be dead. You'll be hanging from that tree out there. Wilson's the only man in camp who might convince the miners that Roberts is lying. And the fool had to get drunk. He started drinking as soon as he heard what Cherry said this morning."

Gale shrugged. "I had an idea he would. He promised me that if I ever hurt his daughter, he'd kill me. This way is as good as another."

"But what are we going to do?" said Morehouse.

"What can we do?" Gale said, and turned to face the marshal. "What would you do, Les?"

"What can you do?" said Larkin, and threw his hands wide.

Gale hit him. Larkin's body slammed solidly against the jail wall and slid down.

"Now what?" said Morehouse. "We'd never live as far as Adams Street."

Gale was already stooping, recovering Larkin's keys. The building was divided in half by an iron grating, the rear portion a cell. Larkin had locked the heavy door in this grating, barring Gale from that hole in the rear wall through which Charley Royer had made his escape.

Morehouse laughed shortly. "I never thought of that." He caught up Larkin's gun and pressed it into Gale's hand. "Let's go."

They squirmed through the hole in the rear wall and sprinted down the alley without meeting anyone. Not until they had gained the hills above the town did they pause for breath."

"Tonight," said Morehouse, as they rested, "I'll get a pair of horses. You want to head south into the ranch country, or do you want to try for San Francisco?"

"Neither," said Gale. "How many of the crews can you trust?"

"Most of them," said Morehouse. "What do they have to do with it?"

"Everything," said Gale. "Nothing has changed. What I want and what has to be done, is right here. Hit out for the nearest camp. Get a horse there and pick up a hundred men. Pick men who own good guns. We're going to cross Roberts' flume tonight."

"You're crazy," said Morehouse. "If you stay around here they'll hang you."

"When we start to cross Roberts' flume," said Gale, "the miners will take sides. With a hundred men around me, I'll be much safer than I have been at any moment since Roberts knew that I had arrived in this country. As soon as it's dark, I'll meet you at the top of Yankee Hill."

Morehouse protested, but Gale went on with his orders. "Send word to Aruup to move the material up to the crossing by ten o'clock tonight. Not sooner. Now get at it. You don't have much time."

"Ward. . . ." said Morehouse, then he shrugged and reluctantly pushed on.

Gale stayed where he was and watched the day wear out. From his timbered covert he had a fair view of the town and could see the river trail. Larkin and four men spurred up it within the first hour. Later, a larger group, headed by Chauncey Burns, rode northward and Gale knew these were Roberts' men.

All afternoon, the country swarmed with men and riders searching the rough hills. But none wasted time looking for him so close to town.

As the shadows lengthened, the hunters drifted back. Larkin was almost the last, sitting astride his tired horse dispiritedly. Losing two prisoners in so short a time had not been good for the man's pride.

With nightfall, Gale shifted eastward toward the rendezvous.

Morehouse had done a good job. Better than a hundred men lay on their guns staring at the small fire marking the camp of Roberts' guards. Gale moved along the line, giving his last minute instructions.

"Make a tight circle. Don't let one of them get through. If word gets back to town of what we're doing, we'll be doing more fighting than working." He picked out a tall, rangy man. "As soon as we get them, Evans, take ten men and guard the trails. If you see anything, shoot. We want plenty of warning. But don't mistake our supply wagons."

Morehouse led one contingent away and Gale worked closer to the fire. He was barely twenty yards away when the shrill whistle broke the night. Roberts' guards were instantly alert. They came to their feet, peering into the dark.

Gale called, "Hold it, boys. You haven't got a chance. Listen." He called louder. "Start counting."

"One," said some man behind him. "Two," the next man echoed. "Three. Four. Five." It went on, the voices swinging around the circle. Before they had reached twenty, the guard captain called, "What do you want?"

"Lay your guns down," Gale ordered, "and line up along the flume."

They obeyed in sullen silence. Gale's crew closed in. Well organized, they secured the prisoners, then seizing their tools, sprang to work.

By the time the first wagon load of material came over the rim, they had ripped the brush and timber from the new right-of-way, and already were digging holes from the stone supports of the trestle, working by the light of flaming tar barrels.

Gale moved up and down the line as wagon after wagon drew in, coming in order, the supports first, the bracing next, the timber for the flume last. Ready-cut, it rose like magic, each piece fitting perfectly, due to Aruup's planning.

As the last wagon dragged up the grade, Roberts' ditch was crossed and only one small section of flume remained to connect with the point where the gravity ditch would take off toward town.

Gale was surprised to see Aruup swing down from the high driver's seat. The merchant, usually dry and taciturn, was more morose than ever.

Gale said, "Cheer up, Emil. My neck feels good so far."

"My neck wouldn't feel good if it were holding up your head," said Aruup. "Running out proved Roberts' case better than anything he could have done in open court. Why didn't you wait and give us a chance, friend?"

"I had my reasons," said Gale, shortly. "Don't you realize if this crossing wasn't made and the ditch completed, that everything will be lost, the money wasted, the bank busted?"

"Everything is lost," said Aruup, quietly. "The bank is busted. Your crossing won't help, Mr. Gale."

"What do you mean?"

The older man looked at him keenly. "I've never questioned you. I'm not questioning you now. All I know is that a man who claims to be a real representative of the House of Rothschild, arrived on the evening stage. He has spoken to Telfair and made his announcement. It appears your friend Telfair is an imposter."

"What happened?" said Gale. "Did Telfair run out?"

Aruup shook his head. "He didn't run. He and Ben Derksen have locked themselves in the bank building."

"You mean they're there alone? Without help?"

"They're without help," said Aruup, and a faint smile twisted his mouth. "But not alone. Ben invited the Rothschild man to stay with them."

Gale turned and yelled to Morehouse and the small man came running. His immaculate clothes were dirty and ruined. The grime of the night's work streaked his face, but he was grinning. "Hey, Emil! What do you think of her?" He gestured toward the trestle. "Roberts is beat now."

"No," said Gale. "We're beat now. I've got to get to town." He told Morehouse quickly what had happened.

"You can't go to town now," said Aruup. "You'll never dare show yourself again. They'd hang you now without even bothering about a trial."

"I can't leave Derksen and Telfair there," said Gale.

"This isn't their fault. I got Telfair into this hole. I'll have to get him out."

"Sure," said Morehouse. "Go on down there and get hung. Don't worry about yourself. Always think of the other fellow."

"What would you do?" said Gale.

"You stay here and I'll go down," said Morehouse. "I got Telfair into this."

Aruup looked from one to the other. "There's no need of anyone going until morning," he said. "The news came too late for the trouble to start tonight. Most of the miners who had come in for the trial have already headed back for their claims. But by morning the news will be around. Roberts will see to that. That's when the trouble will begin. I know you'll both go down there. I know I'll go with you. There are certain things a man just has to do."

4

The sun was well up when the lumbering freight wagons, loaded with armed men, came into Washington and made the turn around the Holbrook House. The news of their approach had preceded them and the swelling crowd, already gathered before the water company office, turned sullenly to stare.

The miners had come in armed and Gale, riding the first wagon, sensed the explosive tension of the throng. Anything could happen. Had he been alone, he knew he would have never gained the bank. It would be touch and go now.

He had a hundred men. There were twenty thousand packed into the Square, but they were leaderless. His hundred were well organized. It all depended on decisions now. He gave the crowd no time to think, no chance to solidify. Deliberately he drove his team against their ranks.

They gave way grudgingly, but they gave, and in their giving lost the initiative.

Roberts rose to the bandstand, shouting at them, demanding Gale. But the second wagon was already turning into the Square. The third team followed at its tailboard.

Then the fourth. And some unknown miner riding this rig looked down and saw a friend.

"Hello, Jake," he yelled. "Come in to see the fun, did you?"

He got his answer and a laugh and Gale used the resulting lull to gain the bank. With Morehouse at his heels he moved quickly through the door and heard Ben Derksen say, "Why I'm glad to see you, Mr. Gale." There was enormous relief in the fat man's voice.

Telfair was unshaven and disheveled. A well dressed stranger sat at the desk. This man, more angry than afraid, came to his feet.

"Are you the head of these pirates?"

"Sit down," said Ben Derksen, wearily. "Why I guess I've told you a hundred times to sit down."

"Let be, Ben," Telfair said. "Let Ward handle this." He wiped the heel of his hand across his tired eyes. "Gale, this is Featherstone. From London. He's a Rothschild man."

"So I've heard," said Gale.

Featherstone said, "Mr. Gale, you people have misused the Rothschild name. You've laid yourself liable to any suit we care to bring against you. What have you got to say for yourself?"

The marks of the night's work showed on Gale's drawn face, but there was almost humor in his voice. "Featherstone," he said, "I'd like to be able to worry about that. But there's twenty thousand men out there in the Square. They're waiting to hang me. Go ahead and sue."

The door behind Gale burst open. Derksen swung his gun around, then seeing it was Kellogg, let the sawed-off weapon sag.

The lawyer, red-eyed and jumpy, paid no attention to anyone save Gale. "Where's Prudence?" he demanded. "What have you done with her?"

Gale slowly shook his head. "I haven't seen Prudence since yesterday afternoon. I have no idea where she is."

"That's right, Wilson," said Morehouse. "I've been with Ward all the time. I haven't seen Prudence."

Kellogg's shoulders slumped. "Then she's gone," he said. "She took my horse and rode away." He looked at Gale, bitterly. "I can't say that I blame her."

Gale backed up against the desk and sat down. Featherstone tried to talk to him, but Morehouse cut him off.

"Let him alone," the little man ordered. "You're so damned concerned about the name of Rothschild. You could make the name of Rothschild honored in every gold camp in California, this morning. All you have to do is step to that door and tell those miners that the Rothschilds will guarantee the payment of their deposits."

"Really," said Featherstone. "Do you expect my house to put up several hundred thousand dollars to save your miserable necks? You're nothing but cheap swindlers, the whole lot of you."

"No," said Telfair, and plopped a ledger down in front of Featherstone. "Here. Look at this. Every dollar is accounted for. All the money which isn't here in this room, is invested in the water company and this bank holds stock in this water company as collateral. As soon as Roberts' flume is crossed, as soon as the remaining four miles of ditch is dug, that stock will be worth much more than face value. Much more than the loan."

Morehouse cut in. "The crossing has already been made. We made it last night. All that remains now is to dig the ditch. All that takes is labor."

In spite of himself, the Englishman was impressed. He studied the ledger sheets with a practiced eye. "Everything seems to be in order on paper. But a bank has no right to make such huge loans solely from deposits."

"Don't blame them," said Gale. "I stole the money. I forced Telfair to make the loan."

Featherstone looked at him, sharply. "And how much stock do you hold in the water company, Mr. Gale? How much do you stand to make when this ditch is completed?"

Gale looked surprised. Morehouse let a peculiar expression turn down his lips.

"Why," said Gale, "I don't own a share. Outside of a few shares sold in Stockton, no one owns a share except this bank."

"And who owns the bank?" said Featherstone.

Gale looked at Telfair. Telfair shook his head. "I don't know. There isn't any stock in the bank. I never thought of it before. I guess the depositors own it, don't they?"

Featherstone looked from one to the other, amazed. "There's something here I don't understand," he said. "If these books are correct, and you're all telling me the truth, it seems that you've built a water company which you don't own and operated a bank in which you have no claim. If this were taken to a court of law, I would guess that the ruling would be that both the bank and the water company would revert to the depositors since theirs are the only funds involved in the transaction. And, if what you tell me about the water company is true, I would say they are very lucky."

"They're lucky enough," said Morehouse. "Telfair and I outsmarted ourselves. Gale had his own reasons."

Kellogg roused himself. "Mr. Featherstone," he said, "this has been a most revealing talk. Whatever else I can say, I can tell you that every dollar that has gone out of this bank has been expended for the water company. Emil Aruup had the spending of it. And there isn't a more honest man in California."

"Wilson," said Morehouse, "now you're talking. You're the one man in camp the miners believe in. Get out there and tell them that as soon as the ditch is finished, not only will their money be safe, but each depositor will have made a profit. You can do it, Wilson. Even now they'll believe you."

"Yes," said Kellogg. "I can do that."

"Well do it," said Morehouse.

Kellogg slowly shook his head, his brooding eyes on Gale. "No. Not yet. I will not speak until you give Ward Gale to those men outside."

"Why I guess we aren't going to do that," said Ben Derksen. "We'll never do that. Not if they tear this building down, brick by brick."

"Listen to them," urged Kellogg, as the clamor grew, outside. "Maybe you've never seen a mob, Ben."

"I've seen them," said Derksen, simply, "but I've never run from one."

The noise increased, and Gale glanced out at the line of armed men Aruup had drawn up before the bank. He was startled to see it give and break. But more startled when he saw Prudence come through. She had Larkin by the arm. Together, they came on in.

"Ward," she said. "Ward. Are you all right?"

"You shouldn't be here," Gale told her. He caught Kellogg's arm. "Get her out of here, Wilson. Get her out of here, quick."

"Wait," said Prudence. "There's no danger now. They know about it. Larkin read it from the bandstand. Here, read it yourself, Ward. You're free."

"That's right," said Larkin, rubbing his jaws and looking at Gale speculatively. "I don't know how she worked it. It's the first time I ever heard of the governor pardoning a man before he was tried."

"I didn't know you had got away," said Prudence, "until Larkin told me. But I convinced the governor you were innocent."

"How?" asked her father.

She looked at him, then looked away. "Well, it wasn't me alone, exactly. But when forty thousand people petition the governor that a man is innocent, there isn't much else he could do except issue a pardon."

"Forty thousand?" said Kellogg. "Petition? You took my petitions?"

"Yes," she said. "I took your petitions. I cut off the top and wrote a new plea asking the governor, in the name of the undersigned, to free Ward Gale, who had been unjustly convicted of a crime he had not committed."

Inside the office there was no sound. But outside, above the medley of noise, one voice rose sharply. "I don't care if he is pardoned. He stole our money. Let's get him."

Prudence stared at Gale, the color draining from her tired face. "What do they mean?"

Gale caught her hand. "There's no time to tell you now. But thanks for what you have done." He turned to Featherstone. "Will you step outside with me?"

"Gladly," said Featherstone, glancing at Derksen.

"Give me a hand, Ben," said Gale, and dragged the office desk through the door.

Only the thin line of Aruup's armed men separated him from the crowd as he climbed to the desk top. A half brick sailed past his ear and shattered the window behind him.

"Go ahead," he said. "Throw another one. You think bricks will get your money back?"

"Hanging might!" someone yelled up at him.

"Go ahead and hang me," said Gale. "See if that gets your money back. You have deposited two hundred and thirty-five thousand dollars in this bank. There's thirty-five thousand left inside. If we pay you off this morning, you'd each receive about fourteen cents on the dollar."

An angry roar greeted him. "Wait a minute," said Gale. "The money isn't lost. Every penny of it is invested in your water ditch. Mr. Featherstone will tell you, if you'll listen to him. He'll tell you the bank's been honestly run. Not one penny has been used for anything except the loan."

"We want our money!"

"You'll get your money as soon as the ditch is finished. Tell them, Featherstone."

The slight Englishman stepped up to his side. "Gentlemen," he said, "I represent Rothschild's. I came here believing these men to be swindlers. But I have been over the books. Everything Gale has told you is true. Mr. Telfair has done a good job. As soon as the water ditch is completed, every depositor in this bank will have made money, rather than lost it."

"Yeah?" shouted someone. "How's the ditch gonna get finished?"

"That's up to you," said Gale. "Last night we did the thing you said couldn't be done. We crossed Roberts' flume. All that's needed now is labor. You men are miners. You're used to working with pick and shovel. Will you give one day of your time to finishing the ditch? It's that near done and it's up to you. Your money and your future depends on it. Now, what will you do? Hang me, or give yourselves a day's work?"

Silence rolled slowly across the crowd. There were shrewd men here who had forsaken profitable enterprises to search for a quicker fortune in the gold fields. Gale's words had cooled their unreasoning temper. And now, from his place on a high wagon, Emil Aruup turned the tide.

"I'll work a day," he yelled. "I'll work a week if I have to. Let's go."

His words were echoed by the armed men about him. Some of the mob took up the shout. In a moment a thousand men had thrown their hands into the air. The crowd

swayed, gave way a little and the protests of Roberts' fol-
lowers were lost in the gathering roar.

"Come on! Let's work."

Gale jumped down from the desk and pushed boldly out
into the crowd. He was the first man up Washington Street.
As he made the turn, the miners falling in behind him, he
saw Matt Roberts and Phil Darlington standing in the alley
beside the saloon, their anger mirrored on their tight-drawn
faces.

11.

FIVE HOURS before they had wanted to hang him. Now as Gale walked along the right-of-way, coordinating the operation, they glanced up, grinning, jovial, bound to him by the common interest of labor shared.

These men had been toughened by long months of work in the gold riddled gulches. It was amazing how much earth they moved, their energies once directed to the task.

All along the four mile stretch, men sweated shoulder to shoulder. Twenty thousand of them. "There'll never be a thing like this again," said Spencer Morehouse, who walked beside Gale, impressed. "Why didn't we think of this before?"

"Sometimes," said Gale, "it's hard to get men to work to their own advantage. Sometimes a man gets a thing stuck in his mind and it blinds him to everything else. You can be proud of this ditch, Spence."

Morehouse glanced at him, sideways. "I suppose so. But I never thought it would all turn out like this. I wish it had turned out better for you."

"All I've done is mark a little time," said Gale.

"You've broken Roberts in Carolina," Morehouse pointed out. "The money for this ditch would have gone into his bank. All the materials came in by way of Aruup's wagons. It was Aruup who profited, not Roberts. Now you can go after Matt's stage lines and boats."

"No," said Gale. "I won't bother about that."

"Then what are you going to do? Kill him?"

"I don't know," said Gale. "Right now I'm tired."

But tired as he was, they drove on into the night. Gale knew that if they stopped, at least half the men would fail to return on the morrow.

At midnight, he and Morehouse stood at the control gate above the crossing at Roberts' flume and listened as the word came back from town, relayed from man to man. "Done! Done! Done!"

"Turn it on, Spence," said Gale. "It's your ditch."

"Kellogg should be here," said Morehouse. "He thought of it first." But he was not displeased to knock the wedges from the holding gate. The water rushed across the new section and into the freshly dug ditch.

"Done," said Gale.

They stood there for an hour, watching the water from the Stanislaus rush past them. Then Morehouse put his hand against Gale and gave him a gentle shove.

"Go home, Ward. It's all over."

Gale did not answer. He turned and walked slowly away from the little man standing there in the dark. All the way down the grade of the ditch, men stood on the fresh banks watching the flowing water. They turned to speak to him, but he did not answer them.

In the greyness of dawn he came at last to Kellogg's house and stood there looking at the dark windows. Then he continued on toward the deserted Square. Unconsciously, he repeated Spencer's words. "It's all over."

Walking aimlessly, he approached the bandstand, hardly conscious of what he did. He was bone tired, beat out, but there was nothing inviting about the Holbrook House with its narrow, stuffy rooms.

He reached the Oak and glanced up at the rope-scarred limb. Yesterday morning, in the bank, he had been closer to it than he was now. The thought brought a humorless twist to his lips. He sat down with his back against the rough bark, feeling a certain kinship with the tree. It stood alone in an empty place.

With his big hands drooping between his knees, he let his head go forward and dozed. But he could not have slept long. The sun was not yet up, the ragged morning mists not yet risen when he opened his eyes and saw the boots standing close beside him.

Slowly, he tilted his head upward and Matt Roberts stared down at him. The man's face was grey-drawn, his voice toneless, yet harsh.

"I could have killed you, Ward," he said. "I sat in my office window and held a gun in my hand for a long time. I had you in my sights. But there was no satisfaction in that. There's too much between us to settle with gunfire. I'm going to kill you with my hands. That's the way I killed Pete, Ward."

Without warning, then, he struck with his heavy boots.

Pure reflex made Gale roll. The boot heel struck the side of his head, but only a glancing blow. The pain brought him sharply awake. He was on his hands and knees when Roberts rushed. Flattening, he rolled beneath the man, upsetting him.

They came up together. Gale planted his feet and waited for Roberts. He was too tired, he had been through too much to carry the fight. Roberts had asked for it. Let him come and get it.

Roberts rushed him. Gale made no attempt to avoid the man. Their bodies crashed together. Gale went back a yard with that impact, but he held his feet. He drove a fist into Roberts' face.

He had long looked forward to this, but now there was no joy in it for him. He fought grimly and doggedly because he had to, because he knew he was fighting for his life. Roberts was savage.

There was no science, no attempt to evade a blow, almost no sound. Their shuffling feet stirred up and marred the packed dirt. There was no sense of passing time. There was nothing save the sound of heavy blows, the panting gasps of shortened breaths.

Roberts' face was almost unrecognizable, bloody and meaty. Gale's arms grew heavier and heavier until it was torment to lift them. Until he thought each blow would be his last.

Roberts stumbled and put his head against Gale's chest, leaning on him. Gale tried to push him away. He couldn't. He swayed sideways then and Roberts fell.

Gale stood over him, forcing his mind to be interested in Roberts' attempt to push himself up. The man failed twice. Finally he managed to come to his knees. He rested there, looking around, facing Gale without seeing him, then began to crawl painfully around the Square, trying to orient himself.

Gale watched him with utter detachment. Then, too weary to move, he sank down against the tree.

Gradually, his mind shook off the fogging exhaustion, but he sat still, having the Square to himself. Roberts had gained his Express Office and disappeared. But now he reappeared, wedging himself erect in the doorway.

The sun's first rays glittered on the barrel of the pistol in Roberts' attempt to push himself up. The man failed with the distance, came forward with short uneven steps until he had crossed Gold and stood in the Square. Here he stopped, each motion deliberate, and again raised the gun.

Gale watched him curiously. There was nothing he could do.

Roberts' first shot struck the bark above his head and Gale remembered how coming into town on Roberts' stage, this tree had caught his first attention. Now it would be the last thing he would see.

Then Ben Derksen's voice filled the Square and the sound of his lumbering tread rushed past Gale. The fat man's shotgun was leveled before him.

Roberts was swinging his gun toward this threat. Gale thought the fat man had gone crazy. Ben kept running right at Roberts. Roberts fired. The bullet, striking Derksen, broke his stride and made him stagger. But he kept on.

Roberts' second bullet dropped him. Ben went first to his knees, then sat back slowly. "Why Matt!" he cried. "I guess you've killed me. Damned these sawed barrels, anyway. With a long gun I'd of got you from across the street."

He pulled both triggers at once. The recoil knocked him flat, but the heavy slugs almost tore Roberts in two.

From somewhere, Gale found the strength to rise and run. He dropped down beside Derksen and the fat man opened his eyes.

"Ben," said Gale. "How bad is it? You didn't mean that."

"It's all right," said Ben. "I had it coming."

"Like hell," said Gale. "You had nothing like this coming."

"Why I guess I can judge that," said Ben, his round face turning grey. "You don't know, Ward. I'm the one who told Prudence you didn't love her. Tell me I lied to her, didn't I?"

Gale stared down at him. "Yes, Ben," he said. "You lied."

"Good," said Ben. He was smiling when he died.

2

From behind the curtained window, Prudence saw Gale stop before the house. She wanted to rush out to him. He looked so weary and slack shouldered and so alone. But it was better that she wait, better that he should come inside and find again what she had so long denied him.

Instead of turning in he moved away, heading for the Square. With one hand she ripped the curtain aside and started to call after him. Then she remembered Cherry Darlington. Blindly she groped back to a chair beside the table littered with Gale's belongings.

She sank down and sat there a long time. There had been so many mistakes made since that night on the river boat and she blamed her pride. Cherry Darlington had pride, but that pride had not prevented the girl from being willing to testify for Gale, no matter at what cost. Analyzing herself, Prudence wondered if, had the positions been reversed, she would have been willing to make that same sacrifice.

She was on her feet in an instant when the step sounded upon the porch. He was coming back. He had changed his mind. He hadn't gone to Darlington's.

"Come in. Ward! Come in."

"It isn't Ward," said Spencer Morehouse, stepping in the door. "I thought I'd find him here. Haven't you seen him?"

"I've seen him," said Prudence. Her voice was lifeless. "He passed the house a while ago. He's gone on to Darlington's."

Morehouse looked at her. "I don't believe that."

"Where else would he go?"

"I don't know," said Morehouse. Then, with an almost studied cruelty, "Do you care?"

"What good would it do to care?" she said.

"Do you love him?" asked Morehouse.

"I've always loved him. I'm a fool, Spencer. I had him and I didn't know it. Look." She turned quickly to the littered table. "I was gathering up his things last night, thinking he'd want them to go away. I found this book. Look on the fly leaf."

Morehouse took the book and read aloud the message Gale had written while pinned behind his dead horse by Charley Royer's bullets. When he finished he looked at the girl. "You fool. What are you waiting for?"

"A lot has happened since he wrote that," she said. "He wasn't interested in Cherry Darlington then."

"Let me tell you about Ward and Cherry Darlington," said Morehouse. "Cherry knew Telfair was a shoe salesman and not a banker. She threatened to expose the whole game unless Ward was nice to her."

Prudence stiffened. "That woman did that?"

"Don't blame Cherry," said Morehouse, sharply. "She liked Gale. I'm afraid she loves him. She's had a rough time, Prudence. At least think kindly of her. I don't know where Ward is, but believe me, he's not at Darlington's this morning."

Prudence stood up. "One thing more, Spencer. What's between Ward and Matt Roberts?"

"Roberts is a thief," said Morehouse, and suddenly found the word distasteful. "He stole Ward's ship and he murdered Ward's brother who was her captain."

Prudence started to speak. A pistol shot cut across the morning stillness. A second and then a third, followed by a shotgun's roar.

Wordless, they both ran into the street. Doors were opening and people looked out as they ran along the block into the Square, both driven by the same fear.

Prudence saw Gale's hunched figure first. Then she saw Derksen huddled at his side. And in the middle of Gold, Roberts lay. She choked, "He's dead!" and raced forward so swiftly Morehouse could not keep up, so that she reached Gale first.

Dropping to her knees beside him she grabbed him by the arm. "Ward! Ward!"

He straightened. He had been sitting, his shoulders hunched down, his head buried against his crossed arms.

"Prudence."

"Ward. Where are you hurt?"

"Hurt?" he said. "I'm all right, Prudence. It's Ben who's hurt. Roberts killed him."

Prudence looked at Derksen and tears came to her eyes. Gale put his arm around her. People drifted into the Square from all sides, the Washington Street deadline forgotten for the moment.

Larkin came, looked down upon Ben Derksen and then moved on toward Roberts, mumbling to himself. Gale paid no attention to the man or the gathering crowd.

"You better go home," Gale finally said to Prudence. He rose and pulled her up.

"Home?" she said. "What's there for me? You passed the house this morning and didn't stop."

He looked down at her. "No," he said. "I didn't stop. I didn't know whether or not there was any use."

"Come," she said. "Let's both of us go and see."

A little sadly, Spencer Morehouse watched them go. Then, with one last look at Derksen, he walked thoughtfully toward the Holbrook House. Just before he reached the door he raised his head and saw Cherry Darlington. The girl stood in the alley's mouth, directly across Washington.

"Spencer," she said, "is Roberts dead?"

"Deader than hell," said Morehouse. "It's as if he were never in this town."

"Phil must have seen it coming," she said. "He put his money on Roberts and lost the bet. He left last night. He won't be back, ever. I need a man to help me run the place."

Without a word Morehouse started toward her. But before he reached the sidewalk's edge, she called out warningly.

"Wait a minute, Spencer. Think. If you cross this street for me, there's no going back."

He smiled at her. "There's nothing over here I want," he said. And without breaking his stride he crossed Washington.

THE END